In an age of settled achievement, when the weather is controlled and men have long since colonized planets under many other suns, Roald Vincent was content to putter along in his job in the Bureau of Cultural Relations.

But with the shocking thunder of a starship braking at the edge of atmosphere, violence erupted into his placid existence and finished it forever.

Hurled into a vortex of subterranean plots and boiling hatreds, Vincent, to his surprise, found himself reacting strongly and violently—as violently as the men whose extremism attacked the very principles of his precious Bureau, and therefore his reason for being alive. . . .

Other titles by the same author:


THE WHOLE MAN

THE SQUARES OF THE CITY

This is an original novel published by

Ballantine Books, 101 Fifth Avenue, New York

# The

# Long

# Result

John Brunner

BALLANTINE BOOKS     •     NEW YORK

Here about the beach I wandered, nourishing a youth
  sublime,
With the fairy-tales of science, and the long result of Time.

—Tennyson: "Locksley Hall"

# The

# Long

# Result

# 1

THE crisis broke on a morning when I was late for work. As I crossed the entrance foyer of the Bureau of Cultural Relations the calendar clock on the far wall was showing 0938 Zone 7—Thursday, 30th February.

There was nothing in itself so wrong about that. In spite of the unkind cracks people circulated about the Bureau of *Poor* Relations, I'd always felt I was doing one of the most fruitful jobs I could have hoped to find, and I enjoyed it enough not to steal time off, so this late arrival was a rare event. Still more to the point, I'd been doing something with which nobody could argue—not even Tinescu, the Chief of Bureau, in one of his peppery early-morning moods.

At least . . . that was what I thought as I made my way up in the elevator, sublimely unaware of the mess into which I was about to be pitchforked.

I opened the door of my office. On the door, neat Anglic script said:

ROALD VINCENT
*Assistant*
OUT

That last word amended itself to read IN as the secretary built into my desk recognized me. I sat down and asked what I had on hand from yesterday.

My own voice came back at me from the tapes: "Pass 61 Cygni 19k for final assay by Integration. Lunch at the Kingdom with Patricia. Call Micky Torres between fourteen and sixteen regarding Epsilon Eridani 8c. The revised findings on it should be through by morning—if they aren't, chase Tomas."

A good plain day's work. I was about to activate the first job, when I realized the secretary was playing blank tape and hissing slightly. Something else was on file. Abruptly Tinescu's voice rang out.

"Roald, get the hell up to my office the moment you arrive!"

*Blazes. Another of his morning moods.* I sighed, told the secretary to go dormant again, and was about to obey the chief's order when the door slid open, and there was Jacky Demba looking uncharacteristically sour.

"You got here, did you?" he said, passing his mahogany-coloured hand through the tight crisp curls on his long head. "Tinescu's been scouring the Bureau for you this past half-hour."

"I know," I said. "Just got it off my tapes. What's it about, and why should he bother you?"

"Called down a minute ago to say would I check that you hadn't already come in and forgotten to signal it. I should hurry along before he burns through the floor."

And he was gone back to his own office before I had time to ask for further details.

So I went up to see Tinescu, blithely thinking this was one of the usual minor flaps which I sometimes suspected Tinescu of generating in order to compensate for the lowly status the Bureau enjoyed among the other inter-stellar Relations organizations and enhance his sense of self-importance. I got the first inkling I was wrong when I entered the room and heard a ringing voice boom from the outside phone. The little picture screen was turned away from the door, of course, towards Tinescu, but I didn't have to see the face to know he was talking to Giuseppe Capra, the Minister for Extra-Terrestrial Affairs.

Coincidence? Or was this connected with the matter he'd

been chasing me for? I devoutly hoped it was coincidence; I had no special ambition to get involved with problems at Ministerial level.

But the conversation was just ending, and all I caught to serve me as a clue was Capra's final furious blast— "You'd better handle it right, or those Starhomers will be laughing behind their hands at us for the next generation!"

That gave me a few moments of misguided relief. My department was primarily concerned with Viridis, not with Starhome, so I assumed that one would fall in somebody else's lap. I was extremely wrong.

Tinescu shut off the phone and fixed me with a glare. Immediately I said, "I'm sorry to be late, Chief. But there was a call for blood donors because of the rocket crash, and they needed my group."

Tinescu had been framing a blast at me. What I said took the fuel out of his jets. Last night's rocket crash—one of the trans-Pacific expresses had lost its engines on take-off—had shocked everybody, and appeals for donors and emergency nursing staff had been on all the newscasts. In an age when human life-expectancy topped a hundred and ten, it wasn't lightly to be thrown away.

"Why the hell didn't you at least call your secretary?" he growled finally, shaking back his mane of lank black hair. "It was a miracle we got this stay of execution . . . Ach!"

I didn't ask what the phrase was supposed to imply. I was used to him dramatizing every minor upset into a full-blown interstellar crisis. I said, "I didn't know I was going to be so badly delayed. But I stopped to talk to the extra-terrestrial who was on board."

*"What!"* Tinescu jolted upright. "Who!"

That really astonished me. I said blankly, "You mean you weren't told?"

"Listen, since before midnight last night I've had my hands full of something else altogether! Who was it?"

"Not one of ours, fortunately. A Regulan—a private visitor." Tinescu relaxed visibly; Regulans were about the toughest life-form conceivable, and a rocket crash wasn't likely to damage one. "I thought I'd better—well—have a few tactful words with him, see if he was angry at what happened. But he seemed not to be. What's more, he's done some good for Regulan-human relations—the rescue teams were full of praise for the way he helped to bring out the casualties."

Tinescu told his desk to make a memo about that for later reference. Half-way through, he glanced up.

"What's his name?"

"Anovel."

"Okay." He leaned back on completing the memo, and fixed me with a beady glare. "Well! You know who I was talking to when you came in?"

"The Minister, wasn't it?"

"Right." The attention light of the phone came on; he spared a moment to bestow some round curses on it in archaic Rumanian and set the secretary to record. "Anybody told you about a Starhomer ship due to ground this morning?"

I searched memory and shook my head. "Normally I'd hear if it concerned my department—"

"Normally!" Tinescu banged a fist down on the squat plastic bulk of the addresser on his desk; for the first time I noticed its calculator-like keyboard was brand-new, contrasting with the worn air of everything else in the room. "It *does* concern you, like everyone else on this weary old planet! Only the addresser threw the memo I sent you into the wrong channel, and it wound up in Casley's office, and he's on furlough, and—ah, to hell. It's happened now and we shall just have to pick up the pieces." He shot a fierce glance at his watch. "Roald, what do you know about the Tau Cetians?"

"Not much." I frowned. "This isn't my line, strictly—"

"Blazes, I'm only the Chief of Bureau! I know what's your line and what isn't! Answer my question, how about that?"

I recognized the danger signs: Tinescu was getting sarcastic, and that meant this was a crisis-for-real, not a crisis-to-shake-up. Baldly I summarized my knowledge in this area.

"They're the first daughter contact. In other words, they weren't contacted by an expedition from Earth, but by one from Starhome—Epsilon Eridani. So far there's been no direct contact between us and them. I've seen a reference somewhere to the establishment of a mission on their planet, and I guess it won't be long now before we have a delegation of them here, too."

"You're *so* right," Tinescu said sweetly. "To be exact, it will be around lunch-time."

*"What?"*

"Listen hard, because if we foul this one up the consequences will—now *I'm* wasting time!" Another look at his watch. "Roald, at about twenty-three hours last night, this Starhomer ship broached normal for Earth. The captain calls through for a landing pattern, receives it immediately—they'd had the courtesy to notify us the ship was due, at least—and then says, 'By the way, I guess I ought to warn you that we have a delegation of Tau Cetians on board and you may have to make some special arrangements to welcome them.'"

"But this is absurd!" I was half out of my chair.

"Maybe. Or maybe the Starhomers just like the idea of making us run around in little circles. But this isn't the half of it. The Starhomers have done their best to tackle the Tau Cetians by themselves, because of the way they feel about Earth—'anything you can do I can do better,' as you might put it. So they've done all the things we usually do, like assigning a courier to the delegation and so forth, but they just aren't *up* to it." Sweat was beginning to shine

13

on his forehead. "They're technicians, primarily. They don't have a Bureau of Cultural Relations, they don't have enough trained interracial psychologists, they don't have *any* of the basic staffs and disciplines we use. And though the captain of that ship only confessed it very grudgingly, we're sure beyond a doubt that the Tau Cetians have proved more than their courier can handle."

"Fast metabolism, aren't they?" Another snippet about Tau Cetians jumped up in memory.

"Very fast. Chlorine-iodine breathers with a subjective time-rate of one point three—a third again as fast as ours and nearly as fast as that of a Regulan breathing fluorine . . . Blazes! You can get all that off the file—I slapped an imperative-reserve on it for you."

I took a deep breath. "Chief, why me? I've hardly done any alien contact work—"

"Hell and *confusion!* Roald, all I'm asking you to do is go out to the port, take over from this courier—the name is Kay Lee Wong—and get them settled at the Ark. And I'm picking on you half because you're least tied up today with urgent work, half because I think you've got the tact to handle it."

Ark—spelt, strictly, AAC for Alien Accommodation Centre. It sounded straightforward enough put this way, but I had a sinking suspicion that it wouldn't turn out that easy in the long run. I said feebly, "Couldn't Jacky or Tomas—?"

"Roald!" Tinescu got up. He was shorter than me, but if he got really furious he liked to tower over other people who were seated. "It's no business of mine if your ambition is limited to supervising trade in sonnets and string quartets from Viridis—you can stick at that job till you rot, for all I care. But you *are* a department head in this Bureau, and this Bureau has had a problem dumped on its doorstep which it has *got* to clean up. I'd go myself for the sake of seeing the thing smoothed over, but I've got Ministers and other parasites on my back."

He slapped the desk with his open palm. The gesture sent a gaily coloured pamphlet sliding to the floor; I hadn't noticed it before. He dived for it and stuffed it into the destructor slot. From his face, he would cheerfully have done the same to me if I hadn't hurried out of the door.

## 2

A good plain day's work! Hah!

I dropped into my own office chair again and punched for filing centre. "Get me the file on the Tau Cetians," I told the autoclerk. "There's an imperative-reserve on it for me."

"Priority noted," the machine said in its irritatingly sweet voice, and I hit the off switch as though it had done me a personal injury.

Frankly, I was smarting under the rebuke Tinescu had given me. No matter how true it was that I was contented in my present work, with no great wish to be promoted to a tougher grade of problems—no matter how unfair it might be to dismiss what I did at present as "trading in sonnets and string quartets"—I retained my original admiration for Tinescu as an able man and a first-rate administrator, and to have him snap at me did hurt.

But—blazes: even if I was the ranking person in the Bureau with free time available, even if the job was a plain and simple one, why couldn't he have picked one of the sixty-odd staff on regular alien contact duty?

I sighed. I'd been assigned, and I'd have to save the arguments for later. I just hoped nothing would go seriously amiss.

So: clear away today's work. I told the secretary to postpone the Viridis items, neither of which was urgent. That left, first, my scheduled call to Micky Torres. A shame to lose that, but I was intending to fly to Cambridge over the week-end and see him personally, so it didn't really matter. I filed a cancel-with-regret at the exchange.

And, second, my lunch-date. I spoke to the secretary again. "Get me a person-to-person call to Patricia Ryder at Area Meteorological Centre, and call me as soon as it goes through."

I didn't wait for the acknowledge. I was too busy rehearsing my excuses to Patricia. She was by far the biggest thing in my life right now, Bureau or no Bureau. I'd never been married because I'd always felt it was a serious project to be undertaken only with children in mind, and somehow—even though I felt I'd had at least my fair share of attractive women—so far I and the current girl-friend had never managed to agree that long enough had gone in looking for the right partner. An early marriage, after all, theoretically implied the daunting prospect of eighty years together, with modern life-expectancy.

But with Patricia . . . maybe the time had arrived. I couldn't be sure. All I did know was that I hated missing this lunch with her, in spite of knowing that I could see her tonight.

The phone said with its inevitable horrid sweetness, "Patricia Ryder is unavailable at Area Met."

Damn! Well, I'd just have to get Jacky to keep the date for me. I shuffled that to the side of my mind and tried to give some serious thought to what Tinescu had said.

Frankly, I didn't like Starhomers much. My impression —borne out by cultural analysis—was that they were jealous of Earth and determined to outdo the mother world in every possible way. Exactly what kind of insecurity had led to this situation, I wasn't entirely sure, but apparently it was reflected in their rigid, almost deterministic and intensively computer-planned social system. Of course, since they were dealing with intractable material when they tried to apply to human beings the same methods that they found so successful in physical sciences and engineering—where no one could doubt their remarkable achievements—they fell down occasionally. Earth's great successes nowadays were in precisely those areas where Starhome was most likely to make errors. This seemed to be the obvious explanation for the dirty trick they were playing on the Bureau—and via us, on the mother world.

And it *was* a dirty trick. We had refrained deliberately from interfering when they contacted the Tau Cetians, in case their jealousy led them to accuse us of trying to muscle in; we'd stood by, and made admiring noises in the intervals of chewing our nails with anxiety lest they foul up the inter-racial situation through ignorance or arrogance. To bring a delegation of Tau Cetians to Earth without prior warning was explicable only on the assumption Tinescu had made; before admitting they hadn't got the experience to complete the job, the Starhomers wanted to see us run in little circles and perhaps make a bad mistake in our own speciality.

There was no denying it: dealing with the Viridians was infinitely more pleasant than either alien contact or the Starhome side of the Bureau.

I heard the flopping sound from my conveyor which presumably announced the arrival of the Tau Ceti file. Before reaching for it, I remembered a couple more items I should tell the secretary.

"Take a memo for tomorrow. I can accept no appointments owing to pressure of work. Make that standard response to non-urgent calls until further notice. And get me a car for eleven-thirty hours."

Then I dipped into the reception box of the conveyor.

There was something else besides the file. There was also a gaudy pamphlet whose arrival must have preceded mine this morning, for sure as hell it hadn't been in the box when I left yesterday. I unfolded it and stiffened.

In bold letters it was headed: THE STARS ARE FOR MAN!

Wording ran in a narrow column down the left of the page. On the right was a picture of an idealized man and woman, both tall and graceful, wearing light spacekit with the helmets thrown back on their shoulders. They were gazing up at a night-black sky in which gleamed a single star of fluorescent ink.

Half sick, half furious, I read the text. *YOU are being robbed—by the fools who have let the harvest of the stars slip away from the rightful owners, HUMAN BEINGS!*

That was how it started. The rest of it was devoted to an attack on BuCult, heavily sown with emotionally loaded terms like *coward* and *incompetent,* concluding with a veiled accusation that we were traitors to our species.

I turned it over. This side bore a cartoon. It showed members of the four most familiar alien races—Regulan, Fomalhautian, Gamma Ophiuchian and Sigma Sagittarian—subtly distorted to appear bestial, helping themselves from a richly stocked storeroom labelled in red letters *TERRESTRIAL KNOWLEDGE,* while a deformed human labelled *BuCult* cowered snivelling in the corner.

Below, there was more text:

*Who discovered starflight? MEN DID!*

*Has any other race a right to take advantage of our achievement? NO!*

*Why should we go on pandering to animals? YOU TELL US!*

*The time has come for men to claim their birthright of SUPREMACY!*

And finally, in small print at the foot of the page: *Issued by the Stars Are For Man League.*

By this time I was almost shaking with fury. I punched the phone for Tinescu's code; when I saw the chief's face, I didn't trust myself to speak, but could only hold up the pamphlet.

"Oh, you've got one of those too, have you?" he sighed. "Put it in the destructor, the way I did. You have work on hand."

"But aren't you going to do anything about it?" I forced out.

"Such as what? The thing crackpot organizations of that sort most dearly desire is to have official status accorded them as a menace. I had the police check on them three years ago, and the report said they were a two-bit cult, better ignored."

"But *blazes!*" I leaned almost into the screen. "This is turning up inside the Bureau! I found mine in the conveyor box. The conveyors don't connect to the outside tubes."

"Oh, so was mine!" he rapped. "I'm having it investigated—but there are a dozen ways someone could get in and plant them, using a trumped-up excuse. Roald, swallow your righteous indignation and get back to those damned Tau Cetians!"

He broke the circuit. I stuffed the pamphlet, as directed, into the destructor slot, and at once regretted not having torn it to pieces first; I felt that strongly about it. Then my watch caught my eye, and I suddenly realized that I had to absorb everything we knew about an entire alien race and prime myself to courier standard in barely an hour and a half.

*Bastard Tinescu* . . . But I slapped open the file.

As I'd expected, it was a randomly compiled, confused mess of assorted facts. The Starhomers simply didn't have our century-long experience to help them organize their data on alien cultures. The photographs, of course, were excellent, and there were plenty of them. Beneath the first which showed a member of the new species, there had been affixed a slip of tactile-true plastic, a Starhomer invention. It was dull, and the date stamped on it showed it was overdue for re-energizing, but I received three distinct sensations when I touched it: firmness, dryness and a slight chill.

The last could be due to the low energy level, or genuine. The environmental data said it was genuine. The Tau Cetians liked an almost sub-arctic climate . . .

I raced ahead as fast as I could go.

None the less, when eleven-thirty overtook me and my car was signalled to take me to the spaceport, I was still far from the end of my self-briefing. I tucked the file under my arm and rose; I'd just have to do the rest in the car.

On the way out, I pressed the annunciator button of Jacky's office, next to mine, and asked if I could see him a moment. He invited me in with a chuckle, having apparently recovered his habitual good humour.

"What did the chief want you for? Bawl you out for being late, hm?"

"Not exactly." I didn't want to chat, just to ask one favour. "He's given me a job that'll tie me up most of the day and I was supposed to have lunch with Patricia at the Kingdom."

"You want me to keep the date for you? It'll be a pleasure. Though the way you cling to that woman, I'm amazed you trust me enough to ask me."

I felt myself flushing, which was ridiculous. I tried to cover my embarrassment with a bantering answer.

"Exposing you to temptation, Jacky—that's what it is. You know I've always had my eye on Madeleine! Well, thanks a million. I must open jets and get to the spaceport."

"Hey!" The call caught me within range of the door's sensors. It dithered with a soft mechanical complaint over the dilemma of staying open or sliding shut again. "Roald, Madeleine and I are giving a little party tonight—

about eight or nine people is all. We start at nineteen-thirty. Would you like to come?"

"Well . . ." I hesitated, wondering whether to invent a previous arrangement for myself and Patricia, in order to have her all to myself for the evening. Then I realized with wry amusement that Jacky was absolutely right—I was clinging to her with as much tenacity as a teenager to his first girl, at the age when one can't conceive of the second time being as wonderful as this first one.

Mistaking the reason for my not answering, Jacky added hastily, "I meant you and Patricia both, of course!"

"Look, ask her over lunch, will you?" I said at last. "If she hasn't set her heart on anything special, she can accept for both of us. Okay?"

"Okay," he grinned, and waved a dark brown hand before bending back to his work.

The door, finding its problem resolved, shut with the mechanical counterpart of a sigh of relief.

3

IN the exact centre of the eight-mile circle of cleared ground which formed the spaceport, there was a smaller concrete circle a mere thousand yards across, founded direct on to bedrock to take the enormous deadweight of the starships. Its surface was blackened and scarred with the ferocious heat of the jets which had settled on it, but the grass around grew green and unmarked.

None the less, there was always a chance of an error developing in the remote controls which took over the visiting ships at the edge of the stratosphere and guided them to a safe and precise Earthfall. For that reason the port buildings crouched back at the very rim of the field, were firmly anchored to rock and mostly hidden below ground, and had walls and roofs all of ten feet thick. Surrounding them was an impenetrable fence, with only three gates to the road.

Word had apparently got around that something special was happening today. The routine traffic handled by the port always attracted a few sightseers, of course; it was a good place to bring the kids for an hour or two in the hope of seeing a Lunar freighter take off, or a ferry bring in a load from one of the mining colonies on Mars or Venus. But nowadays those were Earth's back yard, a matter of mere days away even at sublight speeds. The landing of a starship, though: that was really something!

Moreover, though spring for the northern hemisphere wasn't officially due until tomorrow, the weather men had decided to give us a preview, and it was a warm clear day with three or four high white clouds gleaming in the sunshine.

Consequently the last couple of miles of the journey were a crawl through thousands of close-packed vehicles. The snub, sheathed antenna on the nose of my car wove its search pattern to the accompaniment of the Bureau's official siren—so rarely used, that this was the first time I'd ever been in a vehicle uttering it. The noise drew the stares of the crowd, and fathers held their children up to look at me. I tried to adopt an official expression, but I was frankly worried. I knew that if anything else had gone wrong since Tinescu briefed me he could have called me in the car and warned me, which he hadn't done; nonetheless, my guts were tight with nervous anticipation.

I'd been gazing at the horde of sightseers for some moments before a curious fact penetrated my mind. Among them there was a strong sprinkling of the distinctive red uniform of spacecrew, and that was incongruous.

Most of the spacemen I knew were only too glad to stay out of sight of a port all the time they were between trips.

No time to puzzle over that, though. The car had picked up the halt pattern being broadcast by a police beacon at the nearest gate. Atop the beacon was an illuminated screen saying LANDING IN SIX MINUTES. Even as I looked it changed to FIVE.

A guard in the gatehouse recognized my siren and I thought he was going to cut the beacon so I could pass. Instead, he came doubling out of the door and rapped on my window for it to be lowered.

"Are you from BuCult?" he demanded.

"That's right, and I'm in a hurry," I said. "I'm meeting some aliens. There should be a truck here from the Ark, and a team of technicians—"

"There's been some kind of trouble with them," the guard broke in. "The port director wants you at his office right away."

*Blazes!* It was all I could do to look anxious rather than scared as the guard cut the beacon and gave a verbal order to my car, directing it to the office where they were expecting me. The trip involved a full-speed dive down a ramp to the underground ring road of the port, a half-mile race along a brightly lit tunnel, and a brake-squealing halt in a parking embrasure labelled RESERVE FOR DIRECTOR RATTRAY'S CAR.

There was no one in sight. This close to landing-time, all the port personnel must be at their posts. I could only guess where to go. The first of the near-by doors which I tried gave on to an empty waiting-room. But the second—

I froze in astonishment. This was a small office without windows. On the left stood Director Rattray, leaning against the wall. On the right were two tough young men in port controllers' uniforms; each held a gun, with which they were covering three sullen young men in the

23

middle of the room, wearing shabby casual clothes and defiant expressions.

Rattray straightened the instant I appeared. "Vincent?" he snapped, and on my nod continued, "I was afraid you might not make it here before the landing was due. Frankly I didn't expect anyone from your Bureau to be covering the landing—even if there are aliens aboard, which was news to me this morning, doesn't the courier usually handle them all the way to the Ark?"

"Usually. This is a special case—a first visit, after all." I didn't say anything about the possibility of the Starhomer courier breaking down under the strain, which was uppermost in my own mind. "What did you want me for, anyhow?"

"It looks as though you're not the only welcoming committee," Rattray answered grimly. "These young idiots were in the crowd to watch the landing when your alien wagon drove up with the Bureau name on it. According to them, they didn't do *anything*—but your truck is now in our workshops for some emergency repairs to restore the airtight seal on the afterpart; seven people are hospitalized with chlorine poisoning, and the police are on their way."

"You mean"—I grasped the shred of the implication—"they deliberately crashed our alien wagon?"

"It was an accident!" The nearest of the captives, a gangling fellow of North European extraction, spoke up loudly.

"Quiet, you," said one of the men with guns.

"They claim the collision reflex on their car failed," Rattray amplified. "But one of my techs took a look at the car after the smash, and he says the controls were on manual. Accident or not, they have a charge of reckless driving coming. No one has a right to use manual in a crowd like that."

"I switched when I saw we were heading straight for the

truck," said the gangling man. "And there's no one who'll say different."

"What made you think it wasn't accidental?" I demanded of Rattray. "Why are they under armed guard?"

"Partly because they tried to lose themselves in the crowd. Partly because of these things."

From a table near by he picked up a folder. He shook it. A shower of brightly coloured leaflets cascaded out. I took one and then another and another. All, without exception, were published by the Stars Are For Man League.

"Seen hand-outs like that before?" Rattray asked.

"I sure as hell have," I muttered. "This very morning, as a matter of fact. You think they're worth taking seriously, do you?"

"Why not? Anyone who really believes men could set up an interstellar empire is ripe for psychotherapy, and somebody who commits a criminal act in support of that belief is not just ripe but rotten."

The phone on the office's one small desk sounded. He tapped the switch. Careful not to get in the way of one of the guns, I moved to peer at the screen and saw it was the guard from the gatehouse calling.

"Police got here, director. Want them to come right around?"

"Of course! Why should they——?"

He got his answer from the even tones of the announcer on the PA, giving us the same message that was going out in every building of the port and from speakers at hundred-yard intervals around the perimeter.

"Landing imminent. Personnel in exposed positions lower safety blinds. Crash and rescue crews on red standby, red-red-*red* standby. Secure sound insulation. Spectators are warned that looking at the descending ship without dark glasses may result in partial blindness. Keep your mouths open to equalize pressure caused by the noise. Landing imminent."

"Well, sir?" the guard at the gatehouse murmured.

"They'll have to wait," Rattray sighed. He glanced at me. "So help me, this business had almost driven the landing out of my head. And I particularly wanted to be in the control room during it."

He snapped his fingers at the men with guns. "Coles, Spanoghe! Keep an eye on these three beauties. Don't let them even scratch themselves before I get back, okay? Want to come down to control with me, Vincent?"

"I think I'd better go see about our wagon," I said.

"Well, you can't. Till the landing's over, you won't be allowed to move around on your own—you might open a wrong door and put somebody off his concentration. Have you been in our control room before?"

"As a matter of fact I haven't."

"Take your chance while you have it, then. It's worth watching our remote supervisors at work. This way!"

I picked up one of the glossy Stars Are For Man leaflets and followed him.

At the end of a wide corridor a monitor glared at us from the centre of a panel labelled:

## REMOTE CONTROL CENTRE
*No admission unless by authority*

Rattray put his eye to the scanner; the monitor identified his retinal pattern and the door slid back. We squeezed into the tiny cubicle beyond, the other side of which was also a door.

"Airlock?" I whispered. "What for?"

Rattray shook his head. "Soundproofing. Keep your voice down. I have one of my top men on this job, but even he can be distracted by outside noise."

The inner door had already slid aside. My first reaction was surprise at the smallness of this, the heart of the port.

I'd had a vague impression that it must be like the main computer hall of the Bureau's Integration department. Instead, we emerged into a room not more than twenty feet square. From the walls, broad shelves were built out, covered with switches; four operators sat at them, headphones clasped to their skulls, eyes fixed on green-black cathode display screens. Against each screen was a label: the nearest read VERTICAL, the one on the right LATERAL I, the one on the far wall LATERAL II, and the remaining one was not yet turned on.

The only light came from the screens, and from a tall, square column of plastic, two feet on a side, which rose to a height of five feet in the centre of the floor. Its top yard was translucent and shed a clear greenish radiance in the depths of which gleamed, not far from the top of the column, a single much brighter green pip. After a moment's examination, I caught on. It was a three-dimensional master projection of which the wall screens showed single aspects.

Rattray had gone around the column. I followed him, and found there was a fifth man in the room, seated in a chair facing the projector. His strongly Asiatic features were made ghastly by the green glow.

"Supervisor Susumama," Rattray said in a low tone. "Sue, Roald Vincent of BuCult."

The Supervisor nodded without taking his eyes off the bright pip in the column. Rattray drew me aside.

"That's the incoming ship," he explained softly. "It's just in range of the remotes now—about five hundred and fifty miles above us. The vertical scale is exaggerated compared with the lateral, of course. If you want the true relationship you have to understand the wall screens, and that takes months of intensive training."

I nodded and glanced at my watch. By my reckoning, the landing process was at least due or even overdue to begin. And at that very moment a booming voice with a strong Starhome accent filled the room.

"Earthport One, Earthport One, this is Starship *Algenib*. Are you ready for us?"

The words were faintly sneering, as though with typical Starhomer arrogance the speaker fully expected to be told he had caught the landing supervisor unprepared.

*Starhomer?*

Abruptly the significance of that struck home, and I turned excitedly to Rattray with a question on the tip of my tongue. But he silenced me with a scowl, and I realized that the very air was ringing with the overstrained tension of this unique occasion. Exactly how I'd managed to avoid making the connection before, I didn't know— pure oversight, perhaps, due to my preoccupation with Viridis and dislike of Starhome. But it had been common knowledge for several months that the Starhomers, who had hitherto relied on vessels bought from us, were building their own first starship.

No wonder spacemen had come to join the regular sightseers at the port today, if for the first time a ship built under another sun was due to make its Earthfall!

4

His face impassive as a bronze Buddha's, Susumama spoke to a swinging mike alongside the luminous column. "Earthport One to *Algenib*, we're ready for you. Commence warping-in procedure. Crew and passengers to high-g stations, please."

"Confirm." The Starhomer sounded bored—I imagined, deliberately.

"Declare your effective mass."

"One five one oh two decimal nine six two."

Over 15,000 tons. I tried to picture the effect of that mass crashing out of control on the fragile concrete raft of the port. It would blast the countryside clean at least as far as the horizon and probably beyond. I started to feel that I had as much of a stake in a perfect Earthfall as both the Starhomers and the port staff.

"Remotes on now," Susumama said, and put his hand to the arm of his chair. He pressed down on an oblong, spring-loaded stud of luminous plastic, and there was a tiny click. In the depths of the column before him, the green pip started to descend visibly.

I glanced around, expecting to see the operators at their screen galvanized into frantic activity. But the only change was that the fourth screen had lit, and I could read its label: SHIPBOARD MASTER.

Rattray exhaled gustily and turned to me. "Safe to whisper now, if you have questions," he told me.

"But—"

"You don't think we'd trust fifteen thousand tons of ship to anything but automatics, do you? The human part of the job is already over—unless the automatics fail, and they're stacked in three-way parallel."

It sounded very safe, put that way. I relaxed a bit. "Ah —could one see the ship yet if one were outside?" I ventured.

"Not yet. Not till the main jets fire. Then she'd be as bright as Venus at full. And by landing, slightly brighter than the sun. You heard our warning to the spectators, didn't you? In spite of that, we'll have to doctor a couple of hundred idiots with sore eyes afterwards. We always do."

"Three g's decel for one and a half seconds," the operator at Shipboard Master screen said. "Orienting over the port."

"Check," agreed Susumama. The blip in the column had descended a good hand's breadth, and lengthened visibly.

"Nasty blow at thirty-six thousand feet," reported Lateral I. "Looks like a transcontinental draught been displaced."

"Memo to talk to Met about that," Susumama said.

"Three point three g's decel, continuing," Shipboard Master said.

This time Susumama merely nodded.

There was silence for a long time after that. The blip floated lower in the column. An occasional flash from one of the wall screens made the room bright as air currents caused random reflections fifty miles below the ship. The tension mounted unbearably, like a trickle charge of electricity.

Finally, the blip reached the floor of the projector. I found I was anticipating the ground-shudder which must surely accompany the touchdown of 15,000 tons, no matter how gently. Rattray gave me an amused glance.

"Not yet. Watch."

Susumama kicked a pedal under his right foot. The scale of the column altered completely; the blip returned to its starting-point, and the Shipboard Master screen shone out like a green fire, eerily luminous.

"Standing on her jets at the ten-mile level while we make a final sweep for obstructions," Rattray explained. "It only takes about ten seconds—and here she comes!"

Now the ship was beyond the point of no return. If the remotes failed, nothing could prevent a crash. As though to underline the fact, even through the thickness of the sound-proofing there stole a faint echo of the mighty thunder of the jets.

Slowly—slowly—the blip settled. It was so quiet I could

hear my own breath in my throat. And at last the ground-shudder came, like a miniature earthquake—and the first non-Earthly starship had completed a successful descent.

My face was running with sweat; so was Rattray's. But when Susumama put the main lighting on, his features betrayed no hint of strain at all.

"Very pretty, Sue," Rattray said.

"Not bad. But if Area Met *are* going to bring their fast winds down so low, they might have the courtesy to warn us." Susumama activated his microphone again. "*Algenib,* remotes out!"

"Thank you, Earthport One," the Starhomer acknowledged, and after a momentary hesitation added, "Our ten-mile g readings averaged one decimal one, plus or minus decimal oh four. Quite comfortable."

"About par for the course," Susumama said without emotion, and cut the mike.

"Now *that*," he finished thoughtfully, "was a comment worth hearing."


It was nice to know the supervisor's worries were over. I was afraid mine might only have begun. It was with a surge of relief that I saw through the windshield of my car the familiar blocky outline of the Bureau's alien wagon parked at the entrance to the port workshops a few minutes later. A stocky man in an atmosphere suit stood by the driving cab, and waved a bulky arm at my approach.

"Mr Vincent? I'm Technician Asprey, from the Ark. You must be worried half to death about our truck."

"Did they fix it?" I clambered out of the car.

"Take a look. I have to hand it to these boys—I never saw anybody work under pressure like they do. Half an hour ago, there was a rip in the back of this wagon you could have walked through without ducking your head, and not a gastight seam anywhere. Now it's set and ready."

The base of the passenger compartment was still crumpled, and stains of iodine clung to the unwiped body-shell. But the lines of bright fresh welding everywhere testified to the thoroughness of the repairs.

"Kubishev's inside double-checking the atmosphere mix," Asprey added. "But unless the aliens are going to be offended at some scratches, I guess we're ready to roll."

"That's marvellous," I said from the bottom of my heart. "Have they told you how soon we can go out to the ship?"

"As soon as we're ready. Ah, here's Kuby now."

A man in atmosphere suiting emerged from the airlock at the back of the truck accompanied by a faint, pungent reek of chlorine. He signalled an okay and stumped around to the far door of the driving cab.

"We'll put the show on the road," Asprey grunted, and turned to get in. I checked him.

"Do you have a spare suit for me, by the way? It may be necessary for me to ride with the visitors."

"I thought that was for the courier," Asprey countered, searching my face with sharp eyes.

"The—uh—the courier seems to have been taken ill."

"Really!" No fooling this man; Ark employees couldn't afford to be stupid. I imagined he already had a shrewd idea of the reason why the Starhomers were handling the Tau Cetians' first visit in this hamfisted manner. "Yes, we can fit you with a spare suit okay."

I got back in my car and ordered it to follow the alien wagon out across the field. I had the feeling that millions of eyes were on me—not only literally, because out at the perimeter of the port news cameras with ultra-telephoto lenses were ranked like mantises, but also subjectively. The fourteen hours or so which had passed since the Starhomers so casually announced they were bringing Tau Cetians with them had been pitifully inadequate for the Bureau to make preparations, but it would certainly have been time enough to let the rumours get around.

Tinescu must have enlisted the Minister's aid to keep the news from being officially circulated, I decided. Otherwise all hell would have broken loose.

A corollary to that idea struck me, and I frowned. Was it pure chance—impulse—that had led the three young men to crash our alien wagon? Or had they known in advance that the wagon was on its way? If so, how? Starhomers were as human as ourselves, descended of Earthly stock; you wouldn't ordinarily send alien wagons to meet even the unique and first of their starships.

I shelved that question. I had no data. Instead, I stared at the ship ahead, trying to decide how it differed from the starships I'd seen before. Certainly it did, but though I felt the difference I couldn't pin it down; my engineering knowledge was minimal. The rest of the scene was normal: the crash and rescue tenders moving away along the narrow-straight concrete tracks to the edge of the port, passing the huge and immensely powerful luggers that would hump the vessel to its permanent berth as soon as the passengers and crew were aground, various port officials in fast cars rolling to their appointed stations.

I made a mental checklist. Landing tubes, mounted on out-riggers for additional leverage and maximum stability —still glowing dull red, but harmless. "Cold" atomics had been the first break-through on the road to safe, effective spaceflight. The outriggers themselves, designed to transmit thrust along optimum resultants to the gigantic hull, now resting on the thousands of hydraulic buffers which adjusted to unevenness on the ground. The hull itself, perhaps unconventionally shaped, but . . .

It was no use. I'd have to get some expert to explain the Starhomer design factors to me. As my car pulled to a halt, I glanced around. Asprey and Kubishev were perfectly capable of preparing the wagon for their passengers, and as yet the landing elevator hadn't arrived on its lumbering tracked base, to suckle up leech-fashion to the ship's main lock.

*He'd do,* I told myself, spotting a man in spacecrew red, with navigation officer's star and sextant gleaming on his lapels. I went over and called to him.

"Excuse me, friend. This ship was built on Starhome, isn't that right?"

He glanced at me. He was frowning. "Yes, that's right. We've been expecting her for some while."

"Can you tell me how she's different from our own? I can't pin the changes down."

"Nor can I," the spaceman muttered. "I was expecting something radically unconventional—the grapevine has been humming for months with rumours of a major design breakthrough. But her lines are ordinary enough. Very clean, but orthodox."

He resumed his own scrutiny of the vessel, obviously preferring to ignore me. I shrugged, and went over to the base of the passenger elevator which by now had reached the ship and lifted its telescopic cab-arm to the level of the locks.

The wait for the cab seemed interminable. It had dragged on for a subjective eternity when the note of the elevator's turbine changed and I tautened. Any moment now, I was due to come face to face with the first Tau Cetians to set foot on Earth.

In a way, it was a disappointment. My immediate reaction was to think how much they resembled men in their protective suits. Then I started to take in the differences: the disproportionately long arms, the discoloration of their face-plates thanks to the mixture of gases behind them, their slenderness—allowing for the suits—in comparison with their height.

The cab was large. There were a number of human beings in it with the aliens—among them presumably, the courier, Kay Lee Wong. I stepped forward hesitantly, scanning faces and seeing several sufficiently Asiatic to match the name.

"Ah—I'm Roald Vincent from BuCult," I said. "Which of you is the courier, Kay Lee Wong?"

"I am," said a clear voice, and a girl pushed forward— a girl so tiny she barely reached my elbow. "And what the hell do *you* want?"

5

FOR the next few seconds I could only think of one thing: absurdly, it was that she couldn't have done too bad a job, since she had obviously got over the first hurdle facing a courier. The aliens—there were five of them— could tell her from other human beings, for all their face-plates were turned to gaze at her. If the Starhomers had picked her for her small size, deliberately giving the aliens a physical characteristic by which to identify her more easily, they'd shown unusual good sense.

Then I was overcome by a sensation of rootless terror, and for a moment thought it was genuine before remembering that the file on the Tau Cetians had warned me: they spoke below the human auditory range, and sub-sonics frequently engender futile alarm-reactions. They were simply discussing me among themselves.

I mastered myself with an effort. I was about to curse Tinescu for not letting me know that the courier was a woman; then I realized the Starhomers might well not have mentioned the fact, and anyway it was irrelevant.

I gave her a second and closer look. Now, I saw that her face showed extreme tension and weariness; her eyes were unnaturally bright, probably from some reaction-speeding dope such as chronodrin. This was confirmed by her movements—quick, but contrasted with periods of utter rigidity, like the darting head-movements of a bird.

Hoping that my tact was enough to insure against the anticipated Starhomer resentment of Earthmen muscling in, I said, "I have a wagon waiting for the visitors, and accommodation for them has been arranged at the Ark —the Alien Accommodation Centre. Perhaps you'd like to introduce me to the delegation; then you can take my car and I'll ride to the Ark with—"

"Get out of my way," she said between her teeth. "I've shepherded these people all the way from Tau Ceti, and I'm not going to hand them over now to some damnfool Terran bureaucrat. Where's this wagon of yours?"

"But—"

She stepped forward. At the last possible moment, seeing she was determined literally to push me aside if she had to, I got out of her way. It would make things worse than ever if the first sight the Tau Cetians were treated to on arrival was physical violence between humans. Behind her, I made a frantic signal to Asprey, waiting at the wagon. As I'd told myself a few minutes ago, he was no fool. He gave a nod which the girl saw, but was able to mistake for a greeting to herself, and I knew he was as aware as I was of the risk involved in having a courier here who might explode into bad temper at any moment.

I kept a smile on my face, just in case the aliens were capable of interpreting human expressions, but it didn't reflect my churning emotions.

Fortunately she seemed to regard Asprey and Kubishev as respectable—perhaps because, like most Starhomers, they were technical men. Shortly she came back to address her charges through a sound transformer carried over her shoulder on a strap.

The whole business of disembarking the rest of the

ship's personnel was being held up while people watched the aliens—and me. With commendable politeness they stood back to give the visitors precedence as, moving with a sort of repressed urgency due to the interaction between their fast subjective-time level and fifteen per cent greater gravity here than at home, they followed their courier to the truck and allowed themselves to be shown into the airlock. Having doggedly put on the suit which Kubishev offered, Kay Lee Wong got in with them.

The instant she was out of sight, I moved. I didn't care what comments I might provoke. The courier system was based on the assumption that during the psychologically disturbing experience of a starflight aliens should only have to adjust to the vagaries of one human being, then get the chance to settle down in a specially prepared environment before meeting a wide range of other people. But the Bureau's couriers were handpicked for extreme tolerance, stability and adaptability—they could stand the pace, even if they had to deal with a fast-metabolism species. This girl wasn't up to it.

I ran straight to Asprey, reading in his grave expression the fact that he realized the girl was near breaking-point.

"Is there a phone in your cab?" I whispered, unsure of the sound-insulation of the truck.

"Yes."

"Good. Who's going to take charge of the visitors at the Ark?"

"I think they've briefed Dr bin Ishmael."

"Great!" That was a reliable man; I'd met him some time before. "Well, look—as soon as you're on the road, call him. Tell him to get the courier out of sight of the visitors as soon as they arrive. Make sure there's a medical doctor on hand to shoot her full of pacificum and force-feed her a good meal and put her to bed till she recovers from her exhaustion. We'll find someone to take care of the aliens. Got that?"

Asprey nodded. "He may not like my telling him," he warned.

"The hell. This is a Bureau order and it comes from me. He can take the argument to Chief Tinescu if he likes— maybe to the Minister. Now get going before she becomes suspicious."

Without waiting to see Asprey comply, I doubled back to his own car and ordered it to make for the Ark. As soon as it was rolling I seized the phone and called Tinescu.

With the always-maddening sweetness of the Bureau's robot secretaries, the answer came that Tinescu was out of the building.

"Oh, blast!" I said aloud. The machine on the other end didn't react; oaths weren't part of its programming. "Well, then, record this. Chief, I gather you know about the damage to our alien wagon. That was sorted out in time, but when I met the Starhomer courier—why didn't you tell me to expect a woman, by the way?—she snapped my head off!"

I gave a summary of the facts so far and explained what precautions I'd asked to be taken at the Ark; then I ended, "I'm going to the Ark right away, to smooth over any harm that may have resulted, but I honestly don't know if I can manage it. Get an experienced alien contact man along as soon as you can!"

I cradled the phone and glanced up, realizing the car had halted without orders. Ahead, I saw a police towcar hauling a battered private car out of the gate—the one, presumably, used to crash our alien wagon. Surely that could have waited till I was on the road ahead!

The phone sounded. Tinescu back in his office, maybe. I reached for it, but the caller was Rattray.

"Vincent? I meant to come and join you at the ship, but I was held up explaining to the police about these three slobs we arrested. Sorry. Did it go off all right?"

"Nobody's actually died of it," I said grimly. "But it's a fair mess that's brewing up."

"I'm not surprised. The Starhomers must want to put us on the wrong foot with the new aliens, hm? Feeding their insecure little egos! Look, why I called you—"

The police stop beacon clearing traffic for the towcar cut its beam, and my car shot forward again. "Yes?"

"The charge against these three bastards—what's wrong with your boss, that he won't file a complaint of damage to property?"

"Give me that again slowly," I requested when I'd drawn breath.

"I wanted the police to take them in for deliberately wrecking your truck. But Tinescu has to file complaint. He refused—wouldn't stop to argue, said he had to leave the office right away."

"You haven't just let them go?" I demanded in dismay.

"Of course not! But they've only been booked on suspicion of reckless driving—this bit with the manual controls being cut in. And that doesn't rate lie-detector testing, so they may simply lie their way out from under."

"I think I see," I muttered. "I'll bet money you mentioned this Stars Are For Man League to Tinescu."

"Of course I did."

"He refuses to take them seriously." I explained about the episode this morning, when I'd found some of their literature in my conveyor box, and Tinescu wrote the League off as a crank group to be ignored.

"Cranks or not," Rattray said, "you can't afford to ignore people like that! This is how I look at it. Disregarding the fact that the logistics of interstellar travel make the idea of conquering—let alone *holding*—a galactic empire completely absurd, we have a responsibility to the future. We're the only race we know of, thus far, with interstellar flight. In a sense this gives us power over alien races. But according to what I hear about the Tau Cetians, they're enough like us to have discovered us in another couple of centuries, if we hadn't come to them first! Somewhere, absolutely for sure, there must be a race which has had starflight longer than we have. What happens when our chauvinistic vacuum-brains hit that fact head on?"

"I take your point," I said soberly. "And I hadn't heard that about the Tau Cetians. I assumed from the file they must be fairly close to us psychologically—if they weren't, the Starhomers couldn't have coped even as well as they have. But—"

"Just a second. What is it?"—to someone else, presumably an intruder in his own office. I didn't hear the reply, but it must have been an urgent call, for he came back with blurting haste.

"Vincent, I just wanted to get you to talk to your boss—persuade him to file that charge. Because if he won't play, I shall. I'll have to make it a charge of interfering with the proper conduct of spatial traffic, or something equally specious, but I want a charge that carries compulsory psyching on conviction. That ought to prove how seriously I take these so-called cranks!"

# 6

IN the neutral light of the Ark's reception hall—dim, sourceless illumination designed to serve creatures used to many different solar spectra—I caught the arm of a man in a lab smock. "Did the Tau Cetians get here okay?" I demanded.

"I'm afraid I haven't heard," the man said. "I work in

the Ophiuchian sector myself. If you know who's looking after them I can probably direct you to him."

"Dr bin Ishmael, I think."

"G block, then. Second left, first right. But watch it— it's being put under gas some time today."

It must presumably already have been "put under gas" —filled with air suitable to receive the Tau Cetians. I thanked him and departed at a run.

I passed the hospital, unique in the known galaxy, whose doctors were equally prepared to set a broken leg, help a Gamma Ophiuchian moult his shell, or repair the seared gills of a Sigma Sagittarian accidentally exposed to Earthly oxygen. I passed the air circulation rooms, where thumping generators secreted the gases needed to support our alien visitors. I turned a corner and almost collided with a robot trolley on which were trays of steaming mush, grey-green and repulsive to human eyes but the very staff of life to creatures from Fomalhaut V. I blessed the foresightedness of the Ark's designers, who had made provision for almost every conceivable life-sustaining reaction. Preparing quarters to house the Tau Cetians would chiefly have been a matter of adjusting some controls.

The sealed door of Block G fetched me up short. A suggestive whiff of chlorine made me sure I'd come to the right place. Panting, I pressed the annunciator button and asked for bin Ishmael.

After only a few seconds, the sound of pumps whirring to get rid of the poisonous gas beyond the door informed me that someone was coming. And it was indeed bin Ishmael; he lifted off his helmet to reveal his brown, lined face with its beaky Arab nose.

"Hoo! That's better!" he exclaimed. "Why, you're Roald Vincent, aren't you? I got your message via Asprey. Come up to my room—it's just a step from here—and I'll give you the latest developments."

He shouted an open-up order at a door ten paces along

the corridor, and led the way, shedding sections of his suit as he went. By the time we reached his room he was stripped to the undersuit, and the various pieces were ready for casual tossing into a corner.

The whole of the main wall was lined with microfiles and textbooks, ranging from dogeared classics of the twentieth century dealing with human responses to conditions in space and printed on obsolete woodpulp paper to the very latest works on that contemporary conundrum, the metabolism of the fantastically adaptable Regulans. A duplicate of the Bureau file on Tau Cetians lay open on the desk.

I decided I would probably like bin Ishmael more than our previous casual—purely social—encounters had already made me. Old-fashioned or not, I liked people who had private libraries, and even Patricia—who took the modern attitude that all you needed was access to a good computer memory—couldn't make me change my views.

"It was smart to notify us about that wildcat of a courier," bin Ishmael said, running his hands through his sleek dark hair and rumpling it into untidy waves. "I laid on the medic you suggested, and he confirmed your opinion. Called it the worst case of nervous exhaustion he'd ever seen. She's doped out in the hospital. Barring any allergies which may develop, she'll be fit company tomorrow."

I exhaled with relief. "But what are you going to do about communications till she wakes up? It only just struck me. If that's the Bureau file you have there, the Starhomers haven't passed enough data on the Tau Cetians' language to enable—"

"No problems," bin Ishamel chuckled. "Those beasts are bright. *Very* bright. You presumably know how close their mentality is to the human?"

"Director Rattray, out at the port, said something about

42

them being apt to invent spaceflight for themselves if they'd been left to their own devices."

"Correct. And bang go some beautiful theories about the connection between oxygen-metabolism and the expansive urge . . . Still, that's irrelevant." He briskened. "I was about to say that of course the Starhomers discovered them by accident, and they didn't have any linguists or semanticists with the expedition. Damned few such people on the whole planet, I imagine, as they don't hold with the soft disciplines. So they took the much shorter course of teaching the Tau Cetians Anglic."

"I thought they used subsonics for communication," I objected.

"So they do. The Starhomers threw together some sound transformers and worked the trick that way. Your lady friend had one with her, so I've sent it to our works to be copied. A beautiful engineering job, it looks like. Anyhow, the Tau Cetians are still apparently at the multilingual stage, but they're close enough to an information theory to realize that Anglic—being artifically constrained to relate very closely to reality—would suit them better than one of their own haphazardly evolved natural languages. Oh yes! These are certainly the brightest bunch we've yet turned up."

"Always excepting the Regulans," I pointed out.

"Hmmm . . . well, yes. Though I've never decided whether Regulans are incredibly intelligent or just unbelievably adaptable."

The sense of strain was leaving me. I hadn't managed to do what Tinescu wanted—take over from Kay Lee Wong at the port—but at least we'd averted a crisis on the way here and the visitors were safely in the hands of experts. I might as well go back to the Bureau, in that case. But I lingered to ask one or two more questions.

"What are you going to do with them now?"

"The Tau Cetians? Oh, the usual routine. First off, we'll

study their biochemistry—got to make sure we can feed them while they're here, cure any diseases they may pick up, and so on. At the same time we'll work out a basic vocabulary in some of their own languages to make certain their semantic orientation in Anglic is sound. It damned well ought to be—they have the same general attributes we do, including bisexuality. And then we'll take them on a guided tour of Earth, though I've no idea how long it'll be before Public Relations is ready to lay that on."

"I don't get that," I said. "Why the difficulty? Simply because this is a first visit?"

"Oh no. This ultimatum from the Stars Are For Man League."

My mind refused to produce an answer to that for several seconds. At last I drew a deep breath.

"Look, what *is* it about this League? That's the third time today I've heard mention of it, but I've never run across it before. And what ultimatum?"

"Oh, it's absurd, of course, but as a matter of security we keep tabs on all anthropocentric organizations, and this one has come ahead lately. Got some money behind it from somewhere, apparently. Printed a lot of glossy new literature, for instance."

"Like this?" I fished out the pamphlet I'd brought away from the spaceport.

"Yes, that's one I've seen several times recently," bin Ishmael nodded.

"So—what ultimatum?"

"They sent an anonymous message to say we'd better keep our aliens under careful guard, because they're tired of monsters wandering around unattended."

"But this must surely be a hollow threat!"

"Think we can afford to chance it? The Starhomers are longing to see us mishandle the first Tau Cetian delegation—that's why they're making things deliberately awkward for us. Think of the effects if someone does attempt the lives of a party of aliens! And think how much worse it'll be if the Tau Cetians are involved—a race which as you said yourself was already on the way to eventual spaceflight."

"Yes. Yes, I see all that. I can also see I'm due for an argument with Tinescu. He denies that this League is worth worrying about."

"Let him come and sit in my chair for a while!" bin Ishmael exclaimed, slapping the top of his desk.

"You were telling me about your plans for the Tau Cetians," I reminded him. "Excuse me probing, but this is outside my regular field, and I'm curious."

"Yes, you're more in human colonial work than alien contact, aren't you? I'm surprised to find Tinescu involving you with this . . . Oh, never mind; he must have reasons." He leaned back, gazing at the ceiling.

"Cultural survey missions are the next big step. Got to be doubly sure what is and what is not safe to trade with them. In the way of information, I mean. For instance, the Sagittarians are completely co-operative, as I'm sure you know. Their psychology doesn't include the concept of competition, let alone violence. So we gave them radio-tracers without hesitation, and they found the techniques immensely useful. They have this big thing in silicon-oxygen genetics and tailor living creatures to their own specifications. But to have radio-tracers you need virtually the whole of nuclear physics, and we couldn't give that to a warlike species. Are you with me?"

I was, naturally. He was only rehashing standard Bureau principles which one picked up even without being directly involved in alien contact. We didn't hand over potentially dangerous techniques; equally, we didn't infringe on any major racial goals, for fear of taking the spirit out of the species. In concrete terms, the Tau Cetians would doubtless ask for the stardrive. They wouldn't get it. By the time they'd developed a world language and their own interplanetary ships, they'd almost certainly invent a stardrive of their own—and who could say? It might even be superior to ours, which suffered from all kinds of drawbacks, such as the nuisance of having to use a set of engines once and once only, for some reason I didn't fully understand but which was connected with the effect of stressed-space fields on intra-atomic distances.

There wasn't much more for me to learn here, obviously. I made to rise, but at that moment the phone went and I paused.

"Doc, we've finished with that subsonic converter now—we have the full specs and we're ready to start building some of our own. But since we only have one I thought you'd like it back as soon as possible."

"Thanks very much," bin Ishmael confirmed. "Have it sent to my office, would you?" He cut the circuit and looked at me.

"Before you go, do you think it would be a good idea if the Tau Cetians met an official of the Bureau? Taking away their courier was probably a blow, but meeting you and being told who you are would help cancel that. They don't have too high an opinion of human beings, quite candidly—the Starhomers made a lot of tactless errors in handling them, including the type of people they chose as members of the delegation."

I said slowly, "In what way, especially?"

"Well, you or I would have chosen a couple of scientists and a couple of psychologists, or the nearest available equivalent. The Starhomers picked four high functionaries. Politicians, if you like. The interpreter is the only one who's really caught on, for instance, to the fact that our slow reactions aren't due to stupidity but to our lower metabolic rate." He turned to a cupboard behind him. "Reminds me—I'm running short of chronodrin. Must have some more sent up."

I hesitated. I didn't really want to involve myself—I

had my own work back at the Bureau. But suddenly I remembered all those cracks about my job with "Poor Relations," and came to a decision. It would harm me, even if I wasn't in alien contact, if something went wrong with what was the entire Bureau's responsibility. I held my arm out for the chronodrin shot which bin Ishmael offered.

It wasn't so much of an ordeal as I'd feared. The interpreter —his name was approximately Shvast—was by far the brightest of the five, as bin Ishmael had stated. I had a shrewd suspicion, as I sat in my clammy atmosphere suit amid the dark gases which the Tau Cetians regarded as clean sweet air, that Shvast was censoring the conversation in both directions in order to maintain maximum tact and politeness. One reason for this suspicion was that occasionally his speed of utterance dropped to a mere gabble, instead of the racing compressed grunt the other visitors employed. The top boss seemed to be the one called Vroazh, whom I tried to identify and distinguish from his companions by physical features: the paleness of the flat prehensile pads he used for hands, the plump fat-sacs under each upper arm. I didn't worry about their clothing, though they were sufficiently man-like to wear elaborate garments of several different colours. Next time, the garments might be totally unrecognizable.

Chiefly, we confined ourselves to generalities. Vroazh asked where Kay Lee Wong was, of course; I explained that she was responsible for the trip only, and now the great and wealthy Bureau (I wished that were true!) had taken charge of their well-being. Did the accommodation suit them? Shvast said it did, though certain minor alterations . . . I agreed to put them in hand. Was the food good? Shvast said it was, though the flavour of one dish which had been offered was . . . I made a note to tell the biological people their synthesists weren't infallible yet. Had their belongings reached them safely? Shvast said they had, although a very precious object had been slightly scratched and . . . I promised to have it repaired by first-rate craftsmen.

And that was about that. As soon as I decently could after mention of food had reminded me I'd missed my lunch, I broke it off and took my leave. Outside the airlock, bin Ishmael thanked me warmly for making his job much easier, but I thought that was pitching it too high.

"The way I look at it," I said, "is this. If something goes wrong when it's the Bureau's responsibility, it's going to be harder than it ordinarily is to say you work for it. I'm insuring against that. Take my point?"

"You damned cynic," bin Ishmael said sourly, and began to help me out of my suit.

"No, I mean it," I emphasized. And I did. I was rather offended when he answered:

"Then that makes you worse than a cynic, and I don't know a word for you. Hold still so I can unhitch this seal, will you?"

7

I took a minor and perverse pleasure in not going straight back to the Bureau. I felt I was entitled to my lunch even if I'd missed the conventional time of day for it. Accordingly I told the car to drop me off at a nearby restaurant and sent it back to the Bureau garage by itself.

There were at least two things I'd learned during the morning which I proposed to investigate further. Over a bowl of Israeli fruit soup I contemplated them.

The first item was perhaps the less important. It was one thing for the Bureau to soft-pedal the Starhomers' arrogance in order not to exacerbate relations between them and Earth. It was another matter altogether when they became sufficiently cynical (and my mind flitted back to what bin Ishmael had said) to involve an alien race in a private squabble. I made up my mind to discover why Tinescu—who must ultimately be responsible, if only because the Minister for Extra-Terrestrial Affairs would have looked to him for advice—had allowed the situation to degenerate to such a risky state.

The second item was closer to home. My reaction to the pamphlet which I'd received in my conveyor box this morning had instinctively matched both Rattray's and bin Ishmael's—and they were a lot more directly involved with the realities of interstellar relations than we in Bu-Cult. To write off the Stars Are For Man League as harmless eccentrics was no longer a tenable position. Whether or not the wrecking of our alien wagon was premeditated, whether or not the three—well, slobs, to borrow Rattray's term—had had advance information of the Tau Cetians' arrival, was beside the point; any lunatic-fringe belief which could provoke such action was *ipso facto* dangerous.

I was going to have to file a report on the day's activity. Somehow, by loading the terms in the report, I would have to convince Tinescu he was mistaken. It was a fascinating exercise in practical semantics. I was still deep in the phrasing of it when I approached the Bureau.

With a start, I saw Jacky Demba coming out under the high arched doorway on which the Bureau's motto was engraved in relief—the ancient Greek instruction which has to precede any dabbling in contact with alien races: KNOW THYSELF! He was deep in conversation with an alien. A Regulan, to be exact—a startlingly beautiful creature like all his kind.

And the Regulan, aware of me long before Jacky because

of his super-delicate senses, gave me a nod of recognition. This put me in the most embarrassing position imaginable. The differences by which Regulans recognized each other were far too subtle for any untrained human to identify. For all I knew, this might be the Regulan whom I had talked to this morning, the one involved in last night's rocket crash—or another entirely, whom I'd met only in passing when he came to visit the Bureau ten years back.

I smiled as though I'd instantly remembered the alien's name, and cast myself on Jacky's mercies. He was used to dealing with this species, and doubtless was expert at telling them apart; equally, he would realize my difficulty.

But he didn't—not at once, at least. For he merely lifted a hand to me and said, "Did everything go off all right, Roald?"

"More or less. Where are you off to?"

"I'm finished for the day," he said, faintly surprised.

I checked my watch, and found it was indeed after sixteen-thirty, the usual closing-time. I hadn't realized it was so late. I muttered a private oath.

"Is the Chief still in?" I demanded.

"Yes, I think so—though not likely to stay very late. Waiting for your report, perhaps?" Luckily he didn't follow that question up, but glanced at the Regulan, who was standing to one side and affecting out of politeness not to listen.

"Anovel, this is Roald Vincent, one of my colleagues here at the Bureau—"

I cut in, relieved beyond description. "We met this morning just for a few minutes. I hope you're completely recovered from the effects of the rocket crash?"

"Thank you, yes. It would take something like a nuclear explosion to put a dent in my hide." The Regulan extended the more delicate of his two right "arms" and I shook the eight-fingered "hand" on the end. This species was unfailingly correct in its observance of the social graces.

Like all adult specimens of his kind, Anovel stood some five feet eight or nine in height, and his resemblance to a horse was remarkable. He had the same long, rather sad-looking head, and twin nostril-sheaths rose above his eyes to give the effect of a horse's ears. His skin was a vivid and beautiful blue, while the mane which ran down the nape of his neck was as yellow as a buttercup. He had four "arms," multiply jointed limbs of which two were slender and terminated in the incredibly deft "hands," while the others were muscled like the hindquarters of a Percheron. Purely in deference to Earthly custom, a kilt was belted about his waist and fell to the backward-bending knees of his long legs. He wore nothing else—and indeed did not even need to wear that much, for these paradoxical beasts could be comfortable over a temperature range of at least two hundred degrees, and alone of the known races could utilize oxygen, chlorine or their native fluorine for respiration.

"You've met already?" Jacky said, astonished, and I explained briefly. He nodded comprehension. "I see! Well, you'll have another chance to get better acquainted tonight —I've invited Anovel to my party. I thought he might like to meet the people I've asked. While I remember, incidentally: I saw Patricia over lunch and you are both coming."

A great guy, Jacky. I gave him a smile and apologized for having to dash off, using Tinescu's impending departure as my excuse.

The chief was indeed still in his office, but he wasn't alone. I hesitated on the threshold, even though he'd told me to come in via the annunciator.

"Oh, don't stand there dithering!" he rapped. "Roald, this is Inspector Klabund of the World Police, Pacific Coast District. Just as well you turned up—I gather he wants to talk to you."

Me? What on earth for? But I moved forward obediently

and took a chair to which Tinescu waved me. The inspector was a big man with short brown hair and deep-set brown eyes. I judged him to be eight or ten years older than myself.

"Now, before the inspector starts on you, I'd like to put some questions to you myself. I gather the Tau Cetians got safely to the Ark, so that's all right, but there's this almost hysterical message I had from the port director, Rattray . . ."

He broke off, perhaps reading my expression.

"Hysterical be damned," I said shortly. "Those three young men deliberately rammed our truck. I'm sure of it."

Tinescu shut his eyes and sighed. "I'll save my questions, then," he said tiredly. "That's what Inspector Klabund is here about."

I gave the policeman a startled glance. "But we're not in the Pacific Coast police district!" I objected.

"Correct," Klabund said heavily. "I'm in charge of the inquiry into last night's rocket crash."

Several things clicked together with extreme abruptness in my mind. I leaned forward. "Was it you who brought Anovel here?"

Klabund hid a flicker of surprise. "The Regulan?" he parried. "Why—yes, that's so."

"Then I'm beginning to catch on. Do you suspect that that rocket was sabotaged?"

"You have a remarkably swift mind, Mr Vincent," Klabund answered slowly. "As a matter of fact, I'm relying chiefly on Anovel's evidence at this stage. He maintains that just before the engines exploded—perhaps a tenth of a second earlier—he heard a sharp noise distinct from the roar of the rockets. I brought him here to confirm that his hearing was sensitive enough to make such fine judgements. He passed one hundred per cent."

"He would. Regulans are very amazing creatures. But

—" I hesitated, then plunged on: "But are you saying that someone would wreck a rocket just to try and kill an alien? Why, anyone should know that a Regulan can stand damage that would mash a man to jelly!"

"Someone insanely convinced of the 'natural superiority of human beings' might conveniently overlook that," Klabund countered.

The idea was horrible, but I had to utter it. I said, "You mean we're up against fanatics that won't object to murdering men and women if they can wipe out a few aliens?"

"I daren't go that far. But it looks terrifyingly like it." Klabund glanced at a small notebook on his lap. "Now, Mr Vincent! I gather you found in your office this morning a leaflet issued by the Stars Are For Man League?"

I nodded. "I was so annoyed I called the chief to complain. He said to stuff it in the destructor and forget it— the police had checked on the League three years ago and rated them as negligible."

"That was true—then. Lately, someone has been pumping money into their organization." Klabund scowled. "Was that the first you'd heard of the League, Mr Vincent?"

"As far as I recall. But not the last. The men who rammed our alien wagon at the port today had a pile of their literature in the back of their car."

"Yes, so I understand." Klabund made a note. "Now what is your exact status here at the Bureau, please?"

"I'm the assistant to the Chief of Bureau responsible for human colonial cultural assay."

"Could you make that a bit clearer?"

I glanced at Tinescu, who could have put it more clearly because he was less involved, but Klabund added sharply, "In your own words, for preference!"

Puzzled, but ready to comply, I said, "Well, you know we have two colonies, I presume—Viridis, at 61 Cygni, and Starhome, at Epsilon Eridani. As part of the terms of foundation and support, we're entitled to cultural survey missions there, and there are two departments in the Bureau which analyse the data received: my own, which is mainly cultural, and Jacky Demba's which is mainly technical. We're—well—middlemen. We pass the information on to centres of study which make use of it."

"I see. Now—if I've got this right—your preoccupation with the cultural aspects means you're more involved with Viridis than Starhome."

"Exactly."

"Amplify, please."

"Well . . . Viridis was planted about a hundred and ten years ago by a group of neo-Roussellians who wanted to return to a pre-technological civilization. On Earth they'd become a laughing-stock, of course, but since the sociologists were pressing the government to aid the study of alternative solutions to the problem of organizing a mass society, their colony was approved and subsidized."

"They got on well?"

"Oh yes. About half of our modern music, drama and verse is Viridian in origin. Their society has a—" I fumbled for the right word. "A depth, a richness, which ours lacks."

"You prefer their society to the Starhomers'?"

"Well—yes. Starhome was founded to see how far a technologically oriented society could be driven. Of course in their own way the Starhomers have done exceedingly well: their level of mechanization is amazing. And, naturally, my department deals with the social consequences of this—well—experiment."

"I see," Klabund murmured. "Mr Vincent, have you ever been a member of the Stars Are For Man League?"

## 8

I'D always regarded myself as quick-witted, but the speed of my reaction to that astonished me as much as it did Tinescu and Klabund. Presumably it was the last kick of the chronodrin shot bin Ishmael had given me to bring my subjective time up to Tau Cetian level which enabled me to bite back the furious denial that sprang to my lips. Obviously, the question had been designed to catch me by surprise and force an unpremeditated response. Why?

Logic said: *Klabund's using a lie-dectector on me.*

So, purely as a matter of principle—because I do not accept that society has the right to invade the mental privacy of any sane individual—I shot out my hand across the shiny surface of the desk and swept aside the squat bulk of the addresser, which was large enough to conceal from anyone sitting in my chair something as compact as a lie-detector.

And I was right. A shallow oblong device with lights on the side turned towards Klabund lay exposed; from it, wires fine as spider's webs trailed towards me and down the front of the desk.

Cold anger welled up inside me. I said in my most frigid voice, "Inspector, what's the idea of putting that thing on me without my permission?"

Klabund was embarrassed. He swallowed hard and glanced appealingly at Tinescu. The chief coughed.

"I asked for it, Roald," he said.

"What the hell *for?*"

"Because you're the reason why the conveyor system has been fed League literature."

I digested that slowly. "It doesn't make sense," I said at last.

"No? I wish you hadn't caught on so quickly, Roald—I'd have liked to see confirmation of the denial you didn't get around to making . . ." Tinescu wiped his face with a weary hand.

"All right, I'd better give it to you straight. You've been having trouble with your Starhomer social assay data, haven't you?"

"Of course I have. There's been a shocking delay on processing the 8c material through Integration—if you hadn't sent me to the spaceport, I was going to chase it today and raise a little hell."

"I know. Well, the delays you've suffered haven't been accidental. There's a cell of League sympathizers in Integration—two key programmers included. And they've been weighting the findings of our survey missions with false data. Tomas discovered this some days ago and reported to me; I told him to say nothing until we had a clearer picture of what alterations were being made and the likely reason for such sabotage. Also we hoped—Yes?" Tinescu cocked an eyebrow on seeing that I wanted to say something.

My anger was subsiding; I might have known it would take something really serious to make Tinescu commit such a flagrant breach of good manners as asking for me to be tested on a lie-detector.

"Micky Torres knows," I said. "This was why I was going to call him today—in fact, it's the main reason I'm due to see him in England this week-end. He's been complaining about anomalies in the 8a and 8b data, which we sent him last month. I thought he was being excessively critical, and I had it in mind to soothe him and make him look over the files again. But this of course changes everything. I still don't see, though, how it connects with me."

"I was just about to explain. We hoped that by leaving the League sympathizers alone for a while, we could tempt them into being over-bold. I believe we've succeeded. They began to look around for new recruits, and not unnaturally one of the first people their eyes lighted on was—you."

"Not unnaturally?" I echoed. "Damn it, chief—!"

"Why not?" His tone was bitter. "Roald, you're one of the most talented people in this whole Bureau, and you prefer to spend your time fiddling away with Viridis material, nice soft cosy cultural data, instead of doing what anyone with your gifts damned well ought to do. Which is get stuck into alien contact work and tackle a job with substance!"

"Now look here—!" I exploded.

"Oh, shut up. Even if it's unpleasant, it's the truth. And it's not my personal opinion alone. It's so obvious that even these lamebrained League members spotted it and concluded the only explanation must be that you didn't care to dirty your hands working for alien races. So they took it for granted you were temperamentally in sympathy with them."

Klabund gave a cough. "I don't think there's any point in my staying any longer, is there?" he suggested. I noticed he was avoiding my eyes; Tinescu had tempted him into what was strictly a breach of legal investigatory procedure, and—as one might have expected—he'd taken a dislike to me in consequence, as the indirect cause of his lapse of discretion and the absolutely direct cause of it being exposed. I hoped I wouldn't have any more to do with this brown-haired man, and I was fairly sure he'd keep from further contact if he could.

Tinescu agreed that he should go, and the moment the door had closed I let go the pent-up fury which I hadn't wanted to release in a stranger's presence. I was really amazed at myself, for normally I'd never have talked back to my boss in this violent fashion.

"Now you can say what you like about my preferring to stay in social assay instead of going over to alien contact! But there's one fact you can't deny, isn't there? My department gets run! Have I ever had a foul-up as bad as this one that's just broken on the alien side? The Bureau has let the Starhomers stampede it into a hopeless mess over these Tau Cetians—a delegation brought in without warning, a courier on the verge of a nervous breakdown, and that's probably not more than half the story!"

"Roald!" Tinescu shot to his feet. "Who's in charge of BuCult? Me, or you? If you're so proud of your ability to run a smooth department, try tackling something *difficult!* Name of disaster, I could slot a dozen competent people into your present post—I could put Micky Torres in, straight from college and without even a year's field work. Well, couldn't I?"

"Now Micky Torres is an exception," I countered feebly.

"Exception be—*Ach!*" He thrust his fingers into his lank hair. "He's still twenty years your junior. The point stands: you have no right to accuse me of letting the Bureau be— what did you say?—*stampeded* by the Starhomers, unless you show you could have handled the situation better yourself. I won't deny you might have done. But how the hell am I or anybody to know that unless you come out from your snug little office and prove it?"

Breathing heavily, he sat down. For long moments I think I literally gaped at him, unable to frame words.

"Go home and calm down, Roald," he sighed at length. "And take this with you, hm? It's my impression that everybody has confidence in you except yourself. And if you can see the truth of that, you'll do what I want because you want it too."

By the time I got home to my apartment, I'd added one more accusation to the list Tinescu had fired at me. I wasn't really riled any longer; I'd accepted that the chief must have been under tremendous pressure to avoid putting a foot wrong with the touchy Starhomers, and the strain accounted for his snapping my head off. I was still wound up, of course—losing my temper was such a rare occurrence the let-down took nearly as long as the build-up, and my pulse was running fifteen above normal. But a relaxing hot bath would take care of that, I figured.

It was this additional accusation, which he'd refrained from hurling at me, that mainly engaged my mind. I'd let myself make a stupid error. Presumably because I disliked Starhome and its conceited inhabitants, I'd never looked closely enough at the recent social assay material from it to spot the faked information added between receipt and dispatch. And I should have been sufficiently thorough to detect it long before Tomas did in Integration.

How much of the altered material had related to the Tau Cetians?

At that point I really began to feel ashamed of myself. As the Bureau file had informed me, that race was roughly where we'd been in the nineteenth or twentieth century. They were competent engineers, astronomers, chemists and architects; they were laying the foundations of the more difficult, because "softer," disciplines like psychology. Such a race was potential dynamite. In the last resort I should have been able to say, from the cultural survey missions' reports, that the Starhomers were likely to use their existence as a weapon against Earth. I'd never come out and said so: I'd let it be inferred from other sources.

All right: I recognized my shortcomings and I was determined to make up for them. Why, then, should I not be able to let go of my tension even now that I was lying in this hot tub, being massaged by the automatic rubbers?

The reason came to me with shocking suddenness. I spoke it aloud.

"Of course," I said. "I'm afraid of being killed."

It wasn't logical. But it was powerful. The survival level of a modern man's brain was still at the stage it had reached long ago in the process of evolution, reacting blindly to any threat of danger. Its only concession to progress had been to widen the range of the cues to which it responded, matching the increased span of human life. I could expect a hundred and ten years of healthy, productive existence on current averages; naturally, like anyone in my position I took fewer risks and watched myself more closely than someone who'd subconsciously accepted that he was lucky to have survived his birth.

And what my reflexes had pieced together, obviously, was the suggestion Klabund had made—last night's rocket crash might have been sabotage—with knowledge of the fact that I'd come to the attention of the League which might well be responsible.

*Might!* I stressed the word to myself savagely. I'd be scared of shadows next.

I got out of the tub in a depressed mood and went for fresh clothes. Just as I was dressed, the phone went, and it was Patricia calling. At once I forgot my worries—except that she might be annoyed at me for breaking our lunch date, unavoidable though that was.

But she smiled at me and puckered her lips in a mock kiss close to the camera at her end, then drew back to reveal that she was wearing nothing but an enormous towel.

"How are you, sweet?"

"Better for seeing you." I said. "Look, about lunch—"

"Oh, you don't have to say sorry!" Her eyes widened. "Jacky told me you had an urgent call away—out to the spaceport, I think he said."

"Yes, that's right. I had to go and meet the Tau Cetians, and this wildcat of a female courier from Starhome."

"Running around with another woman, hey?"

"She called me a damnfool Terran bureaucrat, if you *must* know."

Patricia burst out laughing and almost lost control of the towel. "Did you say you were meeting Tau Cetians? I thought they weren't here yet—surely they're the race the Starhomers found before we did?"

"That's right." I summarized the day's events.

"Well, I'm glad you didn't have any worse trouble," she said finally. "Did you manage to find room in the Ark for these aliens?"

"Oh yes, there was no problem there."

"I'll look out for them, then. I pass the Ark on my way to work. Would I see them from the road?"

"No, they're in G Block, round the back of the site. Tonight I shall think of them all snug in bed or whatever they do, and I shall say, 'There but for a kindly Mother Nature go I'."

"Wouldn't you like to be a Tau Cetian?" Patricia teased.

"Of course not. I'd hate to be any kind of alien—principally because if I was an alien I'd find you repulsive, and that would be ridiculous."

"You say the nicest things, Roald—when you remember. Are you coming here to pick me up before we go to Jacky's?"

"I'd love to. Maybe you hadn't better bother getting dressed . . . ?"

"If that was how you wanted to spend the evening, you ought not to have let Jacky invite us." She was chuckling. "No, come around at nineteen-fifteen and you'll find me party-smart."

"Pity," I sighed. "Well—there's always afterwards, isn't there?"

# 9

As things turned out, when I'd finished saying hullo she had to make herself smart all over again—not that she seemed to object to the extra trouble—and we eventually got to the party half an hour late. Madeleine Demba met us at the door: a slender, very pretty woman older than Jacky, of Dutch and Indonesian extraction. They had folded back most of the ground-floor walls, so that Jacky, mixing drinks at a liquor console the far side of the living area, caught sight of us as we came in.

"You're late!" he shouted. "But don't worry, you're not the last. Anovel hasn't arrived—I told him to come at twenty, give everyone else a chance to get acquainted before he turns up to monopolize our attention. Drink?"

As he'd promised, this was a fairly small gathering. I knew two of the others already: one was Helga Micallef, who worked in the Bureau's biochemical section, and the other was Jacky's ten-year-old daughter Janna, busy being on her best behaviour with a pale young man in the far corner.

Then, while Jacky was fussing around Patricia as he always did with attractive women guests, I realized that there was someone else here I ought to recognize. A man in a formal evening tweed suit.

Suddenly the tweeds melted in imagination into the red of spacecrew uniform, and I identified him as the navigation officer I'd spoken to at the spaceport, waiting for the elevator to crawl up to the Starhomer ship. I went across and introduced myself, and found that he remembered our meeting.

"Glad to know you," he said, taking my hand. "I'm Martin van 't Hoff, Madeleine's cousin."

"Did you figure out what was unusual about the ship from Starhome?" I inquired, for the sake of conversation.

"Not yet, I asked one of the officers if I could go on board, but he told me off rather rudely. Starhomers do tend to be big-headed, don't they? Though of course if that ship is a sample of what they can do nowadays, they have every excuse . . . You won't catch that beauty losing herself in deep space!"

"Losing herself?" I echoed. "I never heard of a starship getting lost!"

"Didn't you? Why, we lost the first one we ever built on Earth—out beyond Alpha Centauri, with a crew of ten on board. That was when we found out the hard way that you can only use a stardrive engine once. You see, the drive-fields permanently warp the electron orbits at the centre of the generators—the physical characteristics of the matter from which they're built become irreversibly changed. This is the reason why starflight is so enormously expensive, of course. When a ship has to carry five or six spare engines . . ."

He broke off, eyes widening, and thumped his fist into his palm. "Why, maybe *that's* what—!"

But I didn't hear the rest. A mellifluous chime from the annunciator rang out, and since there was only one guest now due—a very unusual visitor indeed—a dead hush fell and everyone's eyes fixed on Jacky, going to the door.

I realized how right he had been to say the Regulan would monopolize our attention. With the doubtful exception of Helga Micallef, I suspected that no one here had thought of meeting an alien socially before. It was odd to reflect that even a century and more after the discovery of the first alien intelligence, it was still not generally possible for ordinary people of different races to break through the barrier of strange air and strange food.

"Anovel!" Jacky exclaimed. "I'm really delighted you were able to come. Friends," he added, turning and ushering the alien forward, "you probably heard there was a Regulan passenger in the rocket which crashed last night, who did a lot of wonderful rescue work. Well, here he is."

The Regulan seemed to turn a slightly brighter blue, as if blushing—though I knew it must be my imagination. The superb evolutionary process responsible for these incredible creatures would long ago have shed such superficial reflexes.

"Good evening to you," he said pleasantly.

There was a chorus of rather nervous answers. Then, solemnly, Janna got to her feet, all ten-year-old again. She walked up to the visitor and gazed at him in silent wonder.

"Are you a *real* Regulan?" she demanded at last.

I glanced at Patricia with a smile. But she wasn't smiling—her expression was positively frozen. It took it for granted she was afraid Janna's behaviour might offend the alien.

Not a bit of it. The long head simply cocked on one side, and Anovel agreed gravely, "Yes, I am. Are you a real girl?"

Everybody laughed, Patricia joining in a little late, and the moment of tension passed. Jacky introduced Madeleine and the rest of us, then went to the liquor console.

"Do you take alcohol, Anovel?" he inquired.

"It doesn't affect us as it does you, but I like the flavour of your red wine. Can I have some of that?"

"Certainly!" Jacky found and filled a glass, covering his own nervousness with an excess of flourishes. "Tell me," he went on as he offered the drink, "what do you use if you want to forget your cares—a nice bowl of nitric acid?"

"I'm afraid we have no equivalent of intoxication," Anovel answered with a marvellous imitation of a chuckle. "Perhaps the nearest might be what we call darboonja—

a flourine-carbon compound we use to heighten the visual memory."

"Won't you sit down?" Madeleine murmured, offering a chair.

"Thank you, but my knees bend the wrong way for your furniture. I shall be more comfortable on the floor." He chose a spot near the liquor console and dropped in a single complex motion to a relaxed squatting posture. Janna settled beside him and excitedly demanded that he tell her what it was like where he came from.

After that, all other conversation died a sudden death. Everyone gazed at the long, graceful head of the Regulan poised at a quizzical angle on the heavily maned neck. Finally Janna was persuaded to circle the room and say good night. Watching her reluctant progress to her bedroom, Jacky chuckled.

"She'll be boasting about meeting you all next week at school!" he told Anovel, who gave his strange, rather sad-looking smile in reply. It crossed my mind that at least you weren't likely to find a Stars Are For Man League among Janna's classmates.

After that we all enjoyed Madeleine's marvellous food, including Anovel, who explained that—as with wine—though he derived little nourishment from Terran dishes he liked the exotic flavours. It had been established long ago that a Regulan's metabolism could cope with the ingestion of virtually any carbon-based organic substance, and several which weren't carbon-based. Anovel had explained that a rocket crash wasn't likely to do him much damage—for that, you'd need a nuclear explosion. It looked as though poisoning him was equally out of the question.

Later there was music from Jacky's fine collection of tapes, and the evening slid into a mellow haze. During a lull, I glanced around for Patricia, but she wasn't to be seen; I assumed she'd gone into the garden, for the doors were open to the mild spring night and a bird was singing. I felt great. The liquor had taken care of all my former tension. I considered setting off in search of Patricia, but then a casual remark caught my attention and I leaned forward on my chair.

"What time is it?" someone had asked.

I was making to consult my watch, but Anovel answered readily, "It's just gone twenty-three."

Jacky gave him a puzzled glance. "Do you—ah—do you carry a watch?"

"I don't need one. You humans are the only race which uses them. Did you not know?"

"That's right," Helga spoke up. "All the other species we know operate at a constant subjective time-rate. Ours varies. Tell me, Anovel—I've been meaning to ask you. You aren't here on Bureau business, are you? I don't recall seeing your name on any of our lists."

"No, I'm making a private tour—a complete round of the inhabited worlds. I was at Epsilon Eridani before this, and I plan to go on to Sigma Sagittarii."

"How can you do that?" Madeleine asked in amazement.

"I'm with what you call a 'zoo ship'."

Martin, her spacecrew cousin, chipped in. "We hire ships out to research foundations, and they provide transport between worlds for members of the various races with an itch to travel. In return, the passengers offer themselves for study wherever they stop. It's a way of enabling scientists to get first-hand knowledge of other races' metabolisms."

"I know someone who's done that," I said. "A girl who went to study tectogenetics on Sigma Sagittarii."

"Mildred Bilinska?" Helga inquired. "Yes, I know her too."

"Did she enjoy her trip?" Anovel asked.

"She said she'd had a fine time," I answered. "Of course, she was glad to give up living in a suit when she returned. But you Regulans are lucky that way—you aren't bothered."

Anovel used his marvellous imitation of a laugh again. "Yes, we're very lucky in that respect."

"Surely it must take a long time to complete such a trip," Madeleine commented. "Isn't it—well—difficult to spend so long away from home?"

The long head waved in a slow negative. "You see, we live much longer than you. The eight or ten years the trip will take is—you might say really a vacation."

"How long do you live, then?" Jacky exclaimed.

"At our natural rate—breathing fluorine, that is—twelve hundred of your years. Though since our subjective time is faster than yours, of course it seems even longer."

"And how old are you yourself—if it's not a rude question?" Jacky said.

"On your scale, about two hundred. Quite a youngster yet!"

There was a stunned pause. Glancing around, I saw Patricia had reappeared and was sitting by herself on the other side of the room. Anovel drained his glass and rose.

"Well, I have to be back at zoo by morning," he said. "I really must be going—no, I mean it!" He gestured with all four arms to forestall Jacky's objections, and departed amid a flurry of invitations to return as soon as possible.

"That," Helga said to me dreamily, "is a lovely piece of design."

"What?" I hadn't quite seen the point.

"Oh, Roald! Look, he can breathe flourine, oxygen, chlorine or what-have-you with cheerful indifference. He can eat practically anything—and on top of that he lives twelve hundred years. A *lovely* piece of design!"

"With all those natural advantages," sighed Martin van 't Hoff, "they ought to have discovered starflight instead of us." He gazed gloomily into the depths of his current drink.

At that point Patricia came over and sat on my knee, and

for some while we paid no attention to the other people in the room. Finally she pulled away with a sigh.

"I'm glad that thing's gone," she murmured.

"Why? Because I was paying attention to him instead of you?" I grinned at her. "Don't be silly, my sweet!"

She bit my ear casually. "What did he mean—he 'had to be back at zoo'?"

"Of course, you weren't here when he explained." I told her about the zoo ship system, and finished thoughtfully, "You know, it might be fun to make a trip that way. Say to Regulus."

She pulled away from me. "Roald, you can't mean that!"

"Why not?" I was much drunker than I'd imagined. "I'd love to visit Regulus, and if there isn't any other way . . ."

"You mean you'd let yourself be turned into a lab specimen, poked and probed at by all sorts of—"?

The phone shrilled. I half saw Jacky unfold from his chair to go and answer it, but all my attention was on Patricia—as usual. "Say you're joking!" she pleaded with intensity I couldn't account for in my liquor-muzzy state.

"Sure I'm joking," I soothed. "Think I could stand to be away from you for all that time? Of course, if I could take you with me—"

She tore away from me and stood up facing my chair, all the colour draining from her face. My shock of bewilderment and the words I had in mind to speak were cut short by a cry from Jacky.

"Roald! Here—quickly, for heaven's sake!"

The edge of terror on his voice rasped through my personal dismay. I muttered an apology to Patricia, leaving explanations for later, and hurried to the phone. On the screen was the scowling face of bin Ishmael.

"*Finally* we manage to locate somebody! "I've been calling all over town trying to get hold of your boss, but he's—Oh, the hell with that. You'll have to do. Come on over here, and make it fast.

"Someone's tried to murder the Tau Cetians!"

# 10

THE words seemed to explode in my mind like a bomb. They were no less of a shock to everyone else in the room, and a babble of incredulous exclamations followed. I struggled to absorb the horrible fact bin Ishmael had hurled at me, but long before I'd recovered Jacky had seized command of the situation. With a fierce roar he made everybody else shut up; then he fired some crisp questions at bin Ishmael, and rang off with a promise of immediate action.

"Madeleine, get me and Roald a shot of antalc each, will you?" he rapped. He threw off his evening tweed jacket and replaced it with a casual day cape, shrugging it into place with the same movement that served to press the caller button for his car and bring it from the garage to the front door.

"For me as well, please," Helga called, disengaging herself from Martin van't Hoff, who had taken a great fancy to her. "It sounds as though I might be able to make myself useful."

Madeleine brought three little glasses from the liquor console, brimming with anti-alcohol. I gulped mine down, and it felt in my guts as though I'd swallowed a cold breeze. Then I crossed the room to Patricia, who was ostentatiously ignoring me—gazing out into the garden with her lovely face set and expressionless.

"Sweet, I hate to abandon you like this, but from what bin Ishmael said—"

"Frankly," she cut in, "I don't care."

"Patricia!"

"Oh, *go* to your damned aliens if you must! Go and sublimate your feelings with them—or do they make you so much at home you don't need to sublimate?"

The tone in which she delivered that ugliest of insults was the same she might have used in ordering ten minutes' rain over Oregon.

I'd never imagined the day would come when I wanted to slap a woman's face—least of all, that the woman would be Patricia. But I was raising my hand when Jacky's sharp call from behind me broke in on my paralysing rage. The antalc gripped me, cleansing my mind, and I turned away, conscious only of an engulfing wave of despair.

As the car streaked down the night-bright streets of the city, none of us said very much. Helga kept her eyes on the backs of her strong, capable hands, flexing them together. She put several questions to me, which I answered as well as my confusion would let me. At first it was irritating; then I remembered with dismay that thanks to my study of the Bureau file on Tau Cetians earlier today, I probably knew as much as anyone on Earth about them. I was glad I didn't have to face the task confronting Helga and the other biochemists who would be called in. The Starhomers weren't equipped to provide proper data on the aliens' metabolism; the Ark staff hadn't had time yet to accumulate their usual exhaustive knowledge, and as for the Tau Cetians themselves, if they were at a twentieth-century level their medicine was probably still half superstition.

In any case, according to bin Ishmael they were all five very ill indeed.

Jacky kept the car in emergency top. The scattering of

other traffic we met gave us clear passage on seeing the Bureau sign blinking on and off behind the weaving antenna. It seemed little more than moments before we arrived at the Ark.

The confusion here was terrific. Lights had been slung on hastily-rigged poles around the entrance, and a police stop beacon brought us to a standstill among a crowd of running men and women. The noise of an emergency gas generator formed a humming background to the shouting of frantic orders. Either side of the entrance, police cars were parked; farther away, two rescue teams laboured in the glare of a lamp hung to a tree, stowing away oxygen equipment which had proved unnecessary.

A sweating policeman switched off the stop beacon long enough for Jacky to back the car between an alien wagon and a human ambulance; then we all three jumped out and ran into the building.

We weren't challenged until I'd led the way to the airlock of Block G. There, a girl—by her voice, though her airsuit made her shapeless—demanded what we wanted. When I explained, keeping to whispers because red lights signalled EMERGENCY over the sealed door, she told us bin Ishmael was directing operations from his own office.

At first he didn't notice our arrival. He was completely absorbed in the scene depicted on a vision screen linked to the hospital's chlorine ward: suited humans moving awkwardly around tables on which the naked Tau Cetians lay prostrate. When he did glance at us, his face showed no pleasure.

"You got here, did you?" he snapped. "Not before time! And who the hell may you be, incidentally?" he added to Helga.

"Helga Micallef. Bureau biochemist. I thought I'd be useful."

"Damned right. We need twice the staff we have on hand—with these creatures we're just guessing! That's not so much an operation"—with a gesture at the vision screen —"as an experiment! Go down the corridor. The analysis lab is third on the right. They're working on a haemoglobin equivalent in there, so we can give these poor beasts a transfusion. That sound like your line?"

Helga nodded and went out. As the door slid to, a face appeared on the phone, said something excited and incomprehensible about the interpreter, Shvast, and retreated out of range again.

"That's *something,* bin Ishmael said, and heaved a deep sigh. "But we'll need more than that before the night's out."

"What actually happened?" I demanded.

"Somebody smashed one of the ventilator pipes on the outside of Vroazh's room. Oxygen got in, and the poor devils were half burnt alive. You heard Gobind just now, saying they've managed to get Shvast back on his feet—he was farthest from the leak and got off lightest. Apparently he knows something about their first-aid, at least."

On the screen connected to the chlorine ward appeared a familiar figure, moving weakly but able to stand: Shvast, as promised. He began to indicate with gestures what the suited surgeons should do.

Gobind's face reappeared on the phone and unemotionally reported that if the surgeons could keep the casualties alive another hour, they should be able to synthesize the haemoglobin equivalent by then. And vanished as before.

"Another hour," bin Ishmael muttered. "Allah, what a job! It'll be a miracle if it happens. I tell you, Vincent!" he added fiercely to me. "I'm going to have an inquiry into this business. I'm going to raise such a stink as there hasn't been in fifty years. I want to know who in your damned Bureau landed us in this mess, handing us a group of aliens with no biological data, no medicine, no doctor in charge from their own planet . . . Some heads are going to roll, believe *me*." . .

"I'm not on the alien contact side," I protested. "Don't start taking it out on me!"

"No, you're at least here—though what help that is I don't really know. I can't find your boss, I can't find the head of alien contact, the woman with the impossible name—"

"Indowegiatuk," Jacky supplied. It meant something in an Eskimo dialect, they said; I'd never found out what.

"That's her," bin Ishmael agreed. He gazed at the vision screen again, then burst out, "Do you realize we're having to guess the function of the organs in those bodies? If they die under the knife through even an honest mistake, what do you give for the chance of friendly relations with the Tau Cetians? They—"

A booming noise came from the speaker under the screen, making the objects on bin Ishmael's desk rattle. He snapped his eyes shut, wincing.

"That's a scream. We have no anaesthetic for them yet, of course—we've just been praying they'd stay unconscious till we patched them up. Gobind! Gobind!"

But it was Helga who came to the phone in the analysis lab, holding up a flask of something blue and sluggish.

"Anaesthetic," she said. "We think. Have it tried on the worst hurt one first in case there's an allergic reaction or something."

Jacky leaned close to me to whisper, as bin Ishmael issued orders about this new development. "Roald, did he only want someone from BuCult here so he could snap at us?"

"Use your head," I whispered back. "Suppose one of the aliens recovers enough to complain, and there's no one here to make the official apologies!"

"I thought of that. But how are we going to tackle it? We can't just say, "Sorry someone tried to murder you!' "

"What?" bin Ishmael said, turning away from the screen. "Don't you believe it was attempted murder? I do! The evidence is absolutely—"

"Just a second," I interrupted. "We can't tell the Tau Cetians that, can we? It'll make the Ark staff look bad, I'm afraid, but we positively *have* to say it was a mechanical fault—the valves got crossed, or however it might happen."

"I guess so," bin Ishmael conceded. "Though covering up for some bastard's—"

"Sssht! Don't forget Shvast speaks Anglic," I said in horror. "He's got to see we're doing all in our power to put things right. Ah—get him a sight of the rescue workers, for instance; it's an impressive operation you're mounting."

"Shvast's clever enough to tell if we're faking."

"What's going on right now is *not* faked—though some fakery might be a good idea, at that." My mind was in top gear now. "From what I saw of him earlier I think Ambassador Vroazh is the type to appreciate a scapegoat. Let's stage what they'd regard as adequate punishment for some technician's carelessness; pick someone who's due for transfer or retirement, and act it out where they can see it."

"Yes, we might manage it," bin Ishmael said thoughtfully. "There's an atmosphere engineer who's put in for transfer to Australia . . ."

The surgeons broke in to report success with the anaesthetic and to demand quantities sufficient for all the unconscious aliens. Jacky and I sat silent till bin Ishmael had dealt with this request.

The moment he could catch the doctor's attention again, though, Jacky spoke up. "Look, this business of calling it a murder attempt—I've been thinking. Even the Bureau didn't know before last night that Tau Cetians were due to arrive. So how could a murderer—?"

"Doesn't matter," bin Ishmael grunted. "You go look at

the airpipe, and if you can see how it could have been accidentally fractured, I'll—I'll *eat* it. Every yard of it. And who said it was necessarily meant to be the Tau Cetians who died? My guess is that any aliens would do as well."

"But who'd do such a thing?" Jacky demanded.

I almost wanted to scream at bin Ishmael; I knew what his answer would be, and I knew he'd aim it at me, not Jacky.

"I would suggest the kind of people who crash alien wagons—who think aliens are inferior beings—who claim men have a divine right to rule the universe—"

"The Stars Are For Man League?" I said sourly, and to my amazement Jacky swung his dark head.

"The bunch they think wrecked Anovel's rocket?" he blurted.

"They did that too?" bin Ishmael exclaimed.

"Oh, for—!" I could have wrung Jacky's neck. I didn't know where he'd picked up that wild idea—perhaps from Klabund who apparently subscribed to it. "Jacky, a moment ago you were questioning that this here is a murder attempt—now you're tossing wild rumours around like purest gospel. I think we'd better leave bin Ishmael alone. Maybe we can look at this airpipe for ourselves, hm?"

I glanced at bin Ishmael. "Which way do we go?"

"Oh—through G block and straight out. It's not under gas any longer."

11

THE rooms the Tau Cetians had so briefly occupied had been flushed out with moistened air, and we picked our way through charred alien furniture made of substances resistant to chlorine but ready fuel for the more reactive oxygen. Firemen were playing sprays of inert gas on the few still-smouldering embers.

On the far side of the room where I had earlier met Shvast, Vroazh and their companions, an emergency access lock stood ajar. A police floodlight was focused on the opening, and as we went through to the exterior a man in police black came forward to challenge us harshly. We explained our business, and he turned with a curt, "Follow me!"

Through a tangle of forensic equipment he led us to a point on the outer wall of the block where four square metal pipes, supported at intervals of a yard by F-shaped brackets, ran at waist-height towards the gas-generating plant. Half a dozen men clustered here, scrutinizing the pipes carefully. At first I thought they must be examining an unharmed section, for on the side away from the wall—which of course we could see as we approached—the metal was apparently unmarked. But the policeman asked the workers to stand back for a moment, and gestured for us to look at the side nearer the wall.

A jagged hole had been torn in the pipe, a good three inches across.

"But this is fantastic!" Jacky said, stepping back. "How was it done?"

"I wish someone would tell us," the policeman admitted. "Look, the pipes are only inches from the wall yet all the damage is on the inner side. And the wall's untouched, except for a few splinters of the pipe itself. Any ideas?"

"A—a bomb?" I hazarded.

"Out of the question," said one of the men working on the pipe. He wore a night-vision helmet and carried a black-light projector. "A bomb leaves traces—radioactivity or combustion compounds. So far the only substances we've found are due to the action of air on the gas in the pipe. Not a bomb."

"Someone could have cut it with a torch," Jacky suggested. Even I could see that didn't hold water; the metal had been torn outwards from within the pipe.

. The policeman said, "The only possibility, I'd have said, is a solid shot weighing about half a pound. But if you can tell me how to fire a bullet at the side of the pipe nearer the wall without damaging the side farther away, I'd be delighted to know. Anyhow, what became of it? There's nothing scattered round here but the metal from the pipe."

"Why are the pipes exposed like this?" Jacky asked.

A worried middle-aged woman in an airsuit—one of the staff technicians, presumably—answered him. "So we can service them while the accommodation's in use. There are four pipes because the whole system is in duplicate . . . We switched to the spare pair as soon as we found the hole, but it wasn't soon enough."

"Have you an aesthograph with you?" the policeman demanded of the man in the night-vision helmet.

"Think we need aesthograms on this?" the man countered, not looking round.

"Never can tell what may come in useful." He turned to the woman. "Do you keep such things here?"

"Surely—I'll get you one." She hurried off in search of one of the complex devices used in preparing Starhomer tactile-true flat reproductions like the one I'd found on the Tau Cetian file this morning. Rounding the corner of the building, she almost collided with a man looking for us.

"Mr Vincent!" he called. "Dr bin Ishmael wants you to come and have a word with Shvast, please!"


At sixteen next afternoon, my mind still seemed to be stuck in the small hours of the morning. I was due to take the midnight express to England and spend the week-end with Micky Torres; I wished furiously the clock would spin around and get the day over with.

We'd fed Shvast the story I'd suggested. I had no idea if it had convinced him, or whether he'd merely let himself accept it. And we couldn't tell from what he later said to Vroazh and the others. The Starhomers might have saved themselves some trouble by teaching the aliens Anglic instead of learning a native language, but it made it impossible to eavesdrop. Jacky and I had got away at about three, though poor Helga had still been working. Some progress had been made on a transfusion-medium for the Tau Cetians by then, and today's latest news was that all were expected to survive.

Indeed, by now they probably felt better than I did. I'd got home in time to catch some sleep, but I hadn't been able to turn my mind off. I'd lain awake worrying. Then all of today I'd had to face a succession of interrogations, first from the alien contact staff—wanting to know subtle points about Tau Cetian behaviour which I didn't have the training to spot and remember—then from Tinescu.

And that was where I'd fetched up against something I simply didn't understand. Although the inquiry bin Ishmael was threatening would surely lay the blame for the mishandling of the Tau Cetian affair at his door—the Chief of Bureau was ultimately responsible for anything done by his subordinates—I'd acquired the definite impression Tinescu had had no control over the situation.

How was that possible? BuCult was supposed to be *in charge* of all cultural exchange, taking orders from no one except the Minister for Extra-Terrestrial Affairs. We should have laid down inflexible terms to the Starhomers, saying what we wanted them to do before linking the Tau Cetians into our interstellar web of information exchange.

And it hadn't happened that way.

Weary, mystified to bafflement, I dialled for the sixteen o'clock newscast. All five of the Tau Cetian delegation were on the way to recovery—good. The event was flagged as an accident—better still. Inspector Klabund had been assigned to link up three investigations which now became *sub judice* and not open to public comment: the rocket crash, the wrecking of our alien wagon, and the negligence, stress *negligence,* which had endangered the Tau Cetians.

I whistled, not sure that was wise. The obvious associations would be made in too many people's minds. But if that was how the government wanted to handle it, I couldn't argue.

I was out of it now, as far as I could tell.

What I wasn't out of was this disagreement with Patricia. I still couldn't see what I'd done to make her so angry. I'd called her home; she wasn't there. I'd called Area Met, where she worked, and she was "unavailable for personal calls".

Damn!

I tried once more to lose myself in my work. Usually I managed this easily. Today, though, the affairs of peaceful, qausi-primitive Viridis, with its city-state democracy and communal music-making, seemed drab and insignificant. I could imagine human civilzation enduring indefinitely without sculpture in tactile-true plastic, their latest idea, but the possibility of making Tau Cetians hostile to man was fearful.

I was determinedly forging through an analysis of a new departure in Viridian slang, when I had a completely unexpected visitor: the Starhomer courier, Kay Lee Wong.

She wore a mannish cape and breeches of dark red, and her almond-eyed face was strikingly pretty—so much so, I almost failed to recognize her. Her rest had wiped out the masking strain of yesterday. I waved her to a chair.

"I came to apologize for my behaviour yesterday," she began.

I smiled. "There's no need. I'm coming to know what you must have felt like. I had no sleep last night, and this afternoon I've been saying things to my boss which—well, skip that. But what you said to me was nothing in comparison."

"That's very kind of you. I suppose you must understand my special difficulties better than most people. You're responsible for the social assay material from Starhome, aren't you?"

I nodded.

"Then I imagine if you went to Starhome, you'd find everything quite familiar."

"Oh, hardly. Though it would be easier for me, probably, than it is for a Starhomer visiting Earth."

For a moment her face hardened, as though she took the remark as personal criticism. Then she relaxed and gave a soft laugh. "Yes, the free-and-easy surroundings of Earth are a bit unsettling to someone who's used to Starhome. There's a—well—a kind of dedication at home, that makes everyone very disciplined. But of course this hardly applies to someone like yourself who's in a demanding job."

Mentally I cocked my ears. She hadn't just dropped in for a social chat, then; it was unlikely behaviour from a Starhomer on the face of it, and now I was sure. I said, fishing, "Your system certainly has some notable successes to commend it. The *Algenib,* for instance. I was discussing her last night with a spacecrew officer who watched you land."

Again, that tautening of her face. "Did he have any comments? I admit we're extremely proud of her."

"He said it was a beautiful piece of design, though he wasn't able to pin down how she differs from an Earthly vessel."

Ah! I was on to something. I gave silent thanks that Starhomers included the art of deception in the "soft" human disciplines which they claimed were beneath their notice.

The way in which she changed the subject was almost painful. "Mr Vincent, I gather they called you out to the Ark again last night. That was why you had no sleep?"

"Yes."

"I slept through the fuss, of course—very deeply." Her voice was tightening, despite her attempted casualness. "Dr bin Ishmael told me this morning how helpful you'd been . . . You're interested in the Tau Cetians?"

"Indirectly, yes. Though my chief concern is with human colonial affairs."

"So I understand." She crossed her legs and paid some attention to the straightening of her breeches. "You find your work very—ah—fulfilling, I presume?"

"Oh . . . yes, I guess so." I made the statement grudging, in an attempt to force her into the open. I thought this was the point she was probing, though I couldn't yet see why.

"You don't sound very enthusiastic," she commented. Damned right I didn't! I hadn't meant to. And she went on: "Like anyone else, I imagine you'd take a better post elsewhere if one were offered?"

"It's highly unlikely. I've spent most of my working life in cultural exchange, and I wouldn't care to move to another field entirely."

"I see that. You have what you call a vocation. On Starhome we'd say 'preference-aptitude'."

*Oh, come to the point, woman!* And she did.

"In confidence, Mr Vincent, would you consider emigrating to Starhome if conditions were right?"

But this was ridiculous! I spoke my astonishment aloud. "Starhome? There are no openings for me on Starhome!"

"Not at present, true. But we propose to found an organization which will have all the facilities, and more, which your Bureau enjoys, and we're looking for a man suitable to fill the post of Chief of Bureau."

I was so stunned I almost forgot to make myself look as

if I was considering the idea. What call was there to duplicate the Bureau? All our findings were freely available to
anyone, including Starhomers!

"Of course," she went on, "I realize you can't make your
mind up on the spur of the moment. But believe me,
when we say we mean it to be superior to this Bureau, we
can make it so. Our social organization is more efficient
than—well, I don't need to tell you about that."

Blasted Starhomer smugness!

"And our terms are generous. In fact"—she looked me
straight in the eye—"we are prepared to accept the right
man at his own estimate of his value."

This I was going to have to investigate. I said slowly,
"You're right, I can't say yes or no without time to think
it over. Are you staying on Earth long?"

"The turnaround for my ship is ten days. Next week
I'm supposed to make a tour of recruiting stations, checking on immigration figures, but I shall be at this address
until Monday and again from next Friday morning."

She handed me a slip of plastic with the details on it.

"If you come to a positive decision—and I hope you will
—just call me and leave a message. I look forward to seeing you again soon."

And she took her leave.


12


By then it was sixteen-thirty, the time at which the clean-
ing robots moved in on Fridays. Until nine hours on Monday, the Bureau would be virtually dead, apart from the
Integration section whose computers were too precious to

lie idle and had to work the clock around from year's end to year's end.

I left the office to the machines and headed for home, with three things to worry me now—the League, Patricia, and what Kay Lee Wong had told me.

I couldn't make sense of any of them. The idea of a competing body to the Bureau was silly, especially with Starhomers running it. It was some concession to the facts that they'd gone elsewhere to recruit a Chief of Bureau, but trying to get a Starhomer organization built up from scratch was a job I'd not even have offered to Tinescu, myself.

The way in which the League had jumped up in a single day—as far as I was concerned—from the bunch of crackpots defined by Tinescu to a menacing horde of fanatics willing to crash rockets and assassinate aliens was equally incredible.

And last, but not least, I didn't know what the hell had got into Patricia.

I called as soon as I was home. She was in, but the automatic answerer was connected, and when I identified myself I got a chill response from the politeness circuit.

"Sorry, Mr Vincent. Instructions are to accept no calls from you."

It left me staring at a blank screen.

I ran furiously through the events of last night, as though sheer repetition would clear the events which bin Ishmael's shocking interruption had driven down in my memory. I was half inclined to spend this evening, before going to catch the express to England, in a visit to a commercial clearing-house. An hour or two would suffice to re-stimulate the perceptions and give me a knife-sharp replay of what had been said.

And yet . . . paradoxically enough, I didn't feel I'd lost anything significant. I just hadn't seen the point of the things I did remember.

The possibility of losing Patricia brought me to the verge of frenzy. Up till now, I hadn't realized how completely my subconscious had accepted the notion that we were going to make a permanency of our relationship. I dropped into a chair and scowled at nothing.

Was it that I'd threatened—even jokingly—to volunteer for a zoo ship and go off to Regulus? She wasn't that much attached to me, surely! If she'd said it, I'd have been made thoroughly miserable at the prospect of the separation. But I'd have expected her to shrug and wait for someone else to come along. I was nothing special, after all; now was I?

In fact, to be honest, I'd never figured out why she'd got involved with me in the first place. I'd had attractive girls as often as I could reasonably have expected. Patricia, though, was downright spectacular—her body fabulous, her hair a crown of natural gold, her skin without a flaw. My first reaction had been to shy away because the competition for her would be too intense, and my latest—so it seemed was to hang on her every word with tongue lolling.

Ah, to hell with it! I had five hours on my hands before going to the rocketport. Was I going to spend it mooning in this chair—or what?

I jumped up and began to pace the floor. On the third turn I snapped my fingers. Now *that* was an inspiration. I fished out the card Kay had given me and went back to the phone.

She answered in person. She had changed from her mannish day-clothes into typical Starhomer casual wear: a plain black sleeveless jacket and thin white one-piece hose. The starkness of the contrast accentuated her dark hair and eyes against her sallow skin and made me think of a hungry bird.

Not that I could be very interested in her as a woman, with Patricia on my mind. But if I did have time to kill, I might as well try to spend it in resolving one of the other mysteries I was faced with.

"Why, Mr Vincent! You've been amazingly quick in reaching your decision, haven't you?"

For a second she caught me out, and I failed to recognize the note of mockery behind the words. Then I had to chuckle. "Well, not exactly, I'm afraid. The fact is, I realized how little I really knew about Starhome. Secondhand social assay is no substitute for direct experience. Since I have to go to England for the week-end, I wondered whether we could—oh—have dinner together, for instance. And talk a little more about this proposition of yours."

"I think I'd like that very much," she said.

"You're not doing anything, then?" I was coming back from my preoccupation with Patricia, and my normal sensitivity to nuances of intonation told me now she'd been glad to get this call, but was slightly ashamed of admitting it.

She took the plunge abruptly. "No, nothing. Frankly, Mr Vincent, this is my first trip to Earth, and it's even more disorienting than I'd been told. I see there's no shortage of things to do in leisure time, but I simply don't know where to hook on to what's happening."

That was an apt way of putting it. I'd more than once had Starhomers get in touch with me at the Bureau—reluctantly, because only extreme pressure drove them to confess their problem—in order to ask questions that we natives found astonishing. The intense level of committal which Starhome demanded of its people left even their spare time tightly organized. On Earth, boredom swiftly gave way to a sense of helplessness and ultimately, in the worst case I'd seen, to anxiety neurosis brought on by having to make too many unaccustomed decisions. The crisis might be precipitated by something as minor as how to spend the evening: at a dance, or a concert, or having dinner at a restaurant, or taking a girl flying, or—or—or . . . !

I suddenly felt rather sorry for this stranger to my planet. She must have had a gruelling time with the Tau Cetians, and for all that she'd come close to a breakdown, she hadn't actually caved in, which argued a considerable strength of personality. My original prime intention of pumping her about the Starhomer plan to displace BuCult slipped down to second place in my thinking, and I found I was more concerned over how I could best give her examples she could follow on her own for the rest of her stay here.

I took her to the Kingdom more or less automatically; it was my and Patricia's regular rendezvous, but that was a late development—I'd been using it ever since I joined the Bureau, because it was the best restaurant in that part of the city. That it also happened to be convenient for people from Area Met was a bonus, and this evening entailed a consequence which I didn't know whether to take as amusing or annoying. At the table next to ours was one of Patricia's colleagues, who recognized me at once and cocked an eyebrow on seeing me with another girl.

Oh, let it slide. If it was important, there was nothing I could do.

I began to enjoy myself quite quickly. A lot of Kay's off-putting Starhomer arrogance turned out to be a mask for shyness, and when I'd persuaded her to call me Roald she began to relax. Before we'd finished eating we were already involved in a fierce argument about the social value of individual as opposed to communal recreation—I took the stand that the development of initiative was what counted, while she of course maintained the contrary, that integration of the individual into his society was the prime factor.

I was quite surprised by this. How much easier she was to talk to than Patricia! I could treat her as I might have treated an old friend like Jacky or Tomas from the Bureau, and if she found herself defending an illogical position she would just laugh and give up the struggle. All the time I was with Patricia I tended to be agreeing with her, trying to read into every remark the answer she wanted, for fear of antagonizing her. This was refreshingly different . . .

I pulled up short in dismay. What was happening to me? Was I getting disillusioned with Patricia so soon after deciding that here was the woman I wanted to spend the rest of my life with?

Oh, that was absurd. I shook my head and forgot the silly notion.

After dinner, as a concession to her ideas about communal recreation, I took Kay to a public dance and made sure that she obtained a variety of partners. That wasn't difficult; she stood out among the Earthly girls like a pearl in a heap of diamonds. I'd heard it said by experts that the current generation on Earth was the most physically perfect of all time; we'd been selecting for beauty so long, and enjoyed such a high standard of living, that it was inevitable. I reflected that it was also inevitable for our concept of attractiveness to change. Every other woman in sight was tall, impeccably proportioned—slim-wasted, full-busted—and dressed and coiffed with care and taste. Kay looked skinny beside them, but the sinuous grace she displayed when dancing drew the attention of dozens of men, and after a while she started to preen a little. I couldn't blame her. I went off to the bar for a drink.

In a way, I told myself as I sipped, the difference between Kay and Patricia matched the difference between Starhome and Earth. Kay was—not hard; that was a false definition. Tough? Wiry, perhaps, with a personality as firm and flexible as the slim body under her light clothes. Patricia was softer and—well—more cuddly: the product of a society stable enough to flower instead of merely growing.

Starhome was imbued with a revolutionary spirit dead on Earth these two hundred years.

Funny. I'd never thought of it that way before. I was a fit—opposite of misfit—by my own free choice; at least, I'd always imagined so. I'd had an intellectual comprehension of what life must be like on Starhome, because I dealt in the social assay material our survey missions sent to Earth. But before meeting Kay, I'd never considered this obvious and crucial point: that there must be a lot of people who actively approved and enjoyed that kind of life, or else the society simply couldn't survive.

It was getting late. I went in search of her and found her surrounded by a swarm of would-be dancing partners. I told her about my rocket, and suggested that she might like to stay on—the dance didn't close till thirty minutes in the morning, half after midnight.

But she said no, she'd rather I took her home if I had time, so I did. On the way she was bubbling with gratitude for my alleged trouble in giving her such a pleasant evening, and I completely failed to persuade her that it hadn't after all been a chore in the slightest.

At the door of her apartment she turned to me rather shyly. "You've been very nice to me, Roald," she said. "Er —you do things differently from the way we have at home. Isn't it the custom here that if a man takes a girl out for the evening he—they—well, do you expect to kiss me good night.?"

I almost laughed, but fortunately managed to restrain myself. With gravity to match hers, I said. "Yes, that is the—the custom. But it's entirely up to you. If you want to—"

"I believe I do," she said in a small determined voice, and put her arms around me.

Well . . .

Her mouth was cool and firm, astonishingly different from Patricia's; the sliding movement of the muscles on her satiny bare shoulders came as a mute reminder that she was probably as strong as I was—again, not like Patricia. And there, I thought wryly, was proof how heavily I'd fallen for Patricia: thinking about her while embracing another girl.

None the less it was with a sensation of great satisfaction that I went to collect my baggage and proceed to the rocketport. After last night, naturally, I was extremely tired; long before the steady pull of the rocket's acceleration sank me into my couch, I was dozing.

I think I smiled in my sleep.


# 13


BEFORE I had time to activate the annunciator, the voice rang out from beyond the door.

"Come in, Roald. Dump your bag in the usual place. I'll be with you in a moment."

I had to chuckle. Micky had a phenomenal ear for footsteps; he could identify all his friends before he saw them. The door slid aside to reveal him seated at a typer, moving his hands almost faster than the eye could follow.

I'd been here often enough to know my way around. I went into the little annexe kept for visitors and rinsed travel-dust from face and hands. Then I came back as quietly as I could. Micky was copying from a rough draft, and he'd reached the last page.

These rooms were part of the "new" university buildings—already a century old, but upstarts compared with some of Cambridge's really ancient architecture. I sank into a chair and enjoyed the aura of peace which the place exuded.

The walls were crowded floor to ceiling with books and microfilm spools; the range stretched from recently imported Viridian poetry, rather ostentatiously printed with hand-set type on hand-made paper, to a group of three identical red-bound volumes thickly covered with dust. They were copies of Micky's own novel, *Stars Beckoned,* a historical romance about the early days of Venus colonization.

The number of interests this room reflected was fantastic. A theremin stood under the main window, its flex coiled over an antique and fabulously valuable guitar. Rows of loose-leaf binders containing semantic and sociological notes were half-hidden behind reproductions of classical sculpture: a Rodin, a Henry Moore, the Venus of Milo, and Kasneky's *Virtue.*

On the table beside me was a splendidly bound folio volume whose yellowed page-edges indicated that it was made of woodpulp paper instead of everlasting plastic. Curious, I opened it. It was a collection of engravings by a twenty-first century artist called Laszlo Curtin, whom I'd never heard of. They were amazingly good. When I'd leafed to the end, I turned back to the inside front cover to see where Micky had got hold of it. Tacked there with pseudo-magnetic gum so as not to mark the book and spoil its curio value, was a bookplate inscribed with the resounding name of Muguel Fernando José Maria de Madrigal de las Altas Torres.

"Found my Curtin, have you?" Micky said, slapping the cover over the typer. "Mother picked it up in Buenos Aires last month and sent it to me."

I indicated the imposing name. "Is all this you?"

He laughed. "Yes, it's all me. Mother, bless her, is much prouder of my Spanish antecedents than she ought to be, seeing she's mostly Norwegian herself. Still, I suppose anyone who's inherited a long tradition of middle-class socialism can be excused a hankering after the glamour of autocracy. Madrigal de las Altas Torres—sounds like a line from a song, doesn't it?—is where Queen Isabella was born. They had some colourful royalty in Scandinavia too, of course, which makes me wonder sometimes about the lure of the exotic." He folded his ungainly-looking body into a chair facing mine. "However, how are you?"

"Rather bedraggled. I've had a tough couple of days."

Micky clicked his tongue sympathetically. He was tall and bony. His father's night-black hair and jet eyes contrasted with a skin almost milky in its clearness. Somehow the mixture of genes which produced that had also created the nearest thing to a *uomo universale*—I was ready to swear it—that we'd had in a hundred years. He was doing post-graduate research on the staff of the sociology foundation here and writing his doctorate thesis. Though, as Tinescu had rudely reminded me, he was twenty years my junior, he already had a reputation which would allow him to pick his own post when he was ready. On top of that, he was practically unchallenged as an authority on the social evolution of Starhome.

"I have some bad news for you," he went on. "Remember I said there were anomalies in your recent reports from Starhome? Well, they weren't accidents. They look like deliberate fakes."

"I know," I said, and explained what had happened.

"The Stars Are For Man League? Now what would *that* gang want to mess up Starhomer data for?" he wondered aloud.

"You sound as though you know about them."

"Smattering . . . They're eight or ten years old, started in Transvaal among a group of patriarchal back-to-the-Boers. There's a chapter here, of course—universities tend to attract lunatic-fringe organizations—and I think they have members in most big European cities. But then, so do the

Good Earthers, who believe starflight is a direct invitation to the wrath of God and spend their time praying to be spared the vengeance incurred by the impious spacemen—you'd think they'd get discouraged, but no-o . . . Then there are the Brothers and Sisters of the Fruitful Vine, who hold that marriage, clothing and fidelity are sinful, chastity is a crime and even sobriety is—well—socially undesirable. Like body odour. I'm convinced that bunch started as a joke, but it's been one of the most gorgeous jokes in history. I love 'em."

"How come you know so much about these odd cults?"

"Did a survey of them for my bachelor's thesis. You wouldn't credit, in this supposedly sane day and age, how much balderdash is going the rounds. But most of the cults are dull as ditchwater, and so are their tracts, though the Brothers and Sisters have a version of the Song of Solomon for private circulation only, which—Hell, I started to talk about the League, didn't I? I was going to say I thought they were pure hot-air addicts."

"Tinescu had the police investigate them three years ago. They said the same—then. Lately, I gather, someone's been feeding them with funds."

"Then they'll have to be banned, and quickly," Micky said with decision. "See to it, will you?" And with a swiftness that left me gasping, he was on to another subject: a new project to form a folk-music society and rebuild some of the old instruments like saxophones and spinets.

But you could never accuse Micky Torres of having a butterfly mind. He more resembled a bee; he would flit from item to item as his interest waxed or waned, but he examined each one exhaustively before discarding it. I liked him as much as I admired him, and that was a great deal. In the long-lived modern world, the difference in our ages amounted to little—after the rapids of the teens and early twenties, people entered a sort of great lake of shared experience four-score years in length, and we were friends as much as people living on different continents could be.

Tinescu had been wrong, I thought, watching the white nervous face. Micky wouldn't want my job if I transferred to alien contact. He had more sense than to concentrate on a single facet of so huge a task. In fifty years he would have left a mark on history—perhaps altered the social structure of Earth, perhaps created a new art-form, perhaps done for the inchoate field of sociology what unified-field theory did for physics—conceivably, all three. I felt an unworthy but inescapable pang of envy.

"Oh, I don't think I've shown you this," he said, switching subjects once more with the same disconcerting rapidity. He reached behind him and drew out a small, rather tattered volume. He held his hand over the top of it so that all I could see was the picture on the front: a painting of Mars with a spaceship in the foreground.

"What about it?" I said.

"Well—what do you think it is?"

"It's a spaceship, obviously. One of the early pure-rocket models, I presume, though I'm no expert on that."

"Take a look at the date on it. Handle with care!"

I took it gingerly. It was old, and made of woodpulp paper which had been coated with plastic to preserve it; even so it was brittle to the touch. I looked for the date Micky had mentioned, and found it on the spine. It was—1959.

I said, "But—"

And stopped. It was one of the most violent double-takes I'd ever made.

"Correct," Micky said. "There weren't any spaceships flying to Mars in 1959. Someone who'd read *Stars Beckoned* found a whole pile of those in the attic of his grandfather's house: books and magazines describing what was then the future. It must have been a popular form of entertainment, though frankly I'd never realized there was so much of it published."

I turned the pages in wonderment. "Well! What did they think the future held in store for them? Were any of their prophecies accurate? And were they—what d'you call 'em?— astrologers?"

"Heavens, no. They weren't seriously predicting the future—sociology and mob psychology were just getting started then, and I guess that had proved how vain prophecy was without computers and proper manipulative techniques. No, they were just letting their fancy roam a bit. It's a fascinating side-light on the period, though—I think I'll include the material in my thesis, if I can figure out an excuse. By the way!" He jolted upright. "Ought I to offer you breakfast? I keep forgetting the time differential when you come over from the Bureau."

"No thanks. I ate at the airport before I came here."

"That reminds me." He leaned dangerously far backward on his chair and caught at the dangling mike of a recorder, continuing half to me, half to the machine. "I must make a reservation on tomorrow night's express. I'm coming back to the Bureau with you. There's something rather important I have to discuss with Tinescu. Do you want to hear about it now, or later? It is in your department, though for the moment it oughtn't to be noised around."

Since Micky's notion of "rather important" equated to most people's concept of "epoch-making", I tensed. "Now!" I said anxiously.

"Okay, you asked for it. Earth is now second-best."

*"What?"*

"Earth is no longer the leading human-occupied planet. Starhome is."

I knew it was coming. We'd all known for years. But this was the last place and the last kind of occasion when I'd expected to hear the news. I shook my head feebly.

"I'll spell it out," Micky said, jumping up and pacing the room. "I think so far even the Starhomers don't know the balance has tipped—I wouldn't have cottoned on, but that these faked data I mentioned caused me to go back and take a second look at some earlier results.

"Starhome—as you damned well know—is a force-grown society. It's not exactly regimented, but it's sure as hell disciplined. It was planted by the spiritual descendants of the twentieth-century totalitarians. I know that's a dirty word, but it's an accurate description. Their supreme goal is efficiency. It's the most workable compromise ever achieved between the laxity of individual freedom and the rigidity of a corporate state. Most important, it's a far more efficient *basic* design than we have.

"True, we have a very stable society, and for the past two centuries it's been damned nearly perfect. No one starves; no one lacks work if he wants it, no one's forced to work if he doesn't want to; we have negligible crime, so our police go unarmed—and so on. But any society that's stable and not *utterly* perfect is capable of being surpassed. From the beginning Starhome has been dedicated to maximum utilization of its human resources. We shy away from that—we say 'totalitarianism!' and run a mile.

"So long as Starhome was in the pioneering stage, having its teething troubles, as it were, our superiority remained. But we've completed our social evolution—for this cycle, at any rate. Starhome is just starting out. Sooner or later our lead was bound to disappear, and I'm now convinced that it's gone."

I thought irrationally that I could have known this last night. It was implicit in the difference between Patricia and Kay.

Suddenly, I was wondering how it felt to be a citizen of a backwater planet.

## 14

I knew better than to question Micky's assurances. If he said the balance had tipped, the balance had tipped. But I still needed to ram the news home in my mind.

I said, "What brought you to that conclusion, anyway?"

"Well . . . !" He resumed his chair with a wry smile. "Actually I used a matrix I invented myself, which seems to exhibit remarkable stability over a very big range of factors. I can show it to you if you like, but I imagine the Bureau will be putting it through their computers to confirm my results."

"Let it slide, then." I'd seen Micky's matrices; he was happy dealing with two hundred free variables, and I wasn't. "What's it going to mean in—let's say in public terms?"

"That depends absolutely on how soon the Starhomers catch on. They have no techniques for analysing even their own society, of course . . . but there are indications that suggest they suspect the truth. The landing of the *Algenib,* for instance. They may be flying a kite to test the wind there."

"If they don't know?"

"Why, we get a chance to adjust gracefully and make our bows before leaving the centre of the stage. If they do know they'll barnstorm us out of our place in the sun, and there'll be trouble. Of course, there are a hell of a lot of people who do know already, even if only subconsciously."

"Who?"

"The entire population of Earth."

"I see your point," I agreed. It was logical that once a

culture stabilized its members would realize they ran the risk of being outstripped. "Could this be one of the reasons why the League is breaking loose?"

"Oh, surely. They may well be after the last chance to establish an evolving culture on Earth, by breaking the present one apart forcibly. It won't work. They're bucking history."

He stretched out an arm to take a paper from the stack beside the typer. "Here, this is my fundamental equation. For simplicity you can take Earth's cultural index as a constant—unity. In fact the advances and regressions average out over the last hundred fifty years to plus point zero eight."

"As small as that?" I whistled. Anything less than point one was generally regarded as negligible. I studied the equation and arrived at a rough answer in my head.

"With unity," I announced finally. "I get twenty to forty years *ago* as the time when the balance tips to Starhome."

"Near enough. We've postponed it a little, but for the last time now. The next step will likely be for the Starhomers to try and get rid of the cultural survey missions. Remote government—which is what it is, no matter how discreetly we disguise it—won't appeal to them when they realize the facts."

I snapped my fingers as a horrifying recollection jumped up at me. "They *do* know!" I exploded.

"What?" Micky blinked. "Then your survey missions have missed it. Even when I got rid of the faked insertions, I found nothing to prove it in their reports."

I told him about Kay's invitation to me to become Chief of Bureau for a Starhome rival to BuCult.

"So they've decided to take away our lead in the last field where Earth retains unarguable superiority. That fits. And yet——" He bounced to his feet again.

"Roald, they can't have worked it out the way I did——

they haven't got the trained men. They're flying another kite. Ach! And they're going to be proved right. Because don't you see? They must have been hiding the truth from the survey missions, and that takes skill we never suspected they had!"

Correct. Not to mention long-term planning and incredible self-control. But no one would deny that Starhomers had the latter talent.

"So the colonists are taking the initiative," Micky sighed. "Blazes, Roald—it's the United States and Britain all over again!"

I saw the parallel instantly. I saw other things, too. Most strikingly, how the matter of the Tau Cetians fitted in. For generations Starhomers had regarded "soft" disciplines like psychology as of minor importance; doubtless they felt they could tackle contact with Tau Ceti by rule of thumb. When they discovered it wasn't that simple, they reacted characteristically: first, by trying to put BuCult in an impossible position, leading us to make mistakes of our own; second, by instituting a crash programme in order to make good their deficiencies.

"I think Tinescu suspects," I said slowly.

"There's a brilliant man, if you like!" He whirled to face me. "He has a genius for his work. He has fantastic intuition. What makes you think he knows?"

I described my impression that in handling the Tau Cetian business Tinescu had been at the mercy of forces beyond his control.

"Yes! Yes! Yes!" Micky punctuated the words by driving his fist into his open palm. "My guess is, Roald, that in a year or eighteen months at most the Starhomers will make a showdown of it. If Tinesu has been giving in to them, it's almost certainly because he didn't want to antagonize them and make them declare themselves before we were prepared. Lord, isn't a year a short time?"

He hesitated. "Hell, I think I'd better move to the Bureau, don't you?"

"What about your doctorate?"

"Oh, damn my doctorate! If this goes off properly, they'll be giving me degrees right left and centre *e causis non disputandis*—for unarguable reasons. Think of what's to be done, after all. We must reconcile Earth to its back seat—we'll have to get the Starhomers' cultural exchange working—"

"We will?"

"Don't we owe it to other races to ensure that Starhome is better in *all* respects than Earth? And there's work to do on Starhome too, to prevent their pride of achievement turning into the megalomania that breeds cults like the Stars Are For Man League . . ."

Listening, I felt a mood of calm certitude, as though impersonal destiny had spoken to me. This, I told myself, is going to be Micky's—no: Miguel de Madrigal de las Altas Torres's claim to a place in history. It may take a thousand years for his work to be recognized, and of all the people I know only Anovel will live to see that. But it is definite.

A shiver of cold awe went down my spine. Words with a silent ring of truth came into my mind.

*I am in the presence of the first human being to whom all aliens will be grateful—and acknowledge their gratitude.*

It was a tremendous, majestic sensation to see that it was possible to create a world in all ways better than Earth; perhaps to set an example for Starhome to follow when, in the very far future, it must itself give place to a culture which arose to surpass it. To be conscious of doing something to shape the long result of human history—it was a feeling close to delirium.

It drove everything else out of my mind. It wasn't until I was climbing into the bunk assigned to me aboard the homebound rocket late on Sunday night that I remembered I hadn't called Patricia.

Well, I could call as soon as we touched down. But somehow it didn't seem all that important.

We'd had to take a paired compartment, because we'd left it very late to make our reservations, but at least we had bunks and not merely relaxers. Through the tightly stretched curtain which divided the little room into halves, I heard Micky also climbing into bed. I wished him good night, and some time later dropped into a light doze.

At first I dreamed incoherently of finding my own name in something that served the purpose of a history book but was not actually a book as such. This was pleasant and gratifying, and when I looked further and found Micky's name there in black letters twice as big, I reminded myself, stirring in half-wakefulness, that this was only just. Below the surface of sleep I looked for the name again.

This time, though, it was growing—looming up from the thing which was not a book: a long flexible black shape, which reached out abruptly and clamped over my face.

I was suffocating!

I panicked awake, and found the sensation was real. I strained wildly to draw breath; then, for the first time, my naturally quick reactions saved my life.

Something soft, warm and slippery covered my face, from the bridge of my nose to my chin. It was perhaps as big as my two hands together. With my grasping for breath it had begun to ooze into my nostrils—and that was that told me the truth and enabled me to breathe out with the tiny volume of stale air my lungs still held. It was a sobbing choking gasp, a horrible sound, but it served the purpose. The mass entering my nose drew back, and I wrenched a hand from under the cover and clamped a grip on it.

It tried to writhe away, but I forced my finger-tips between it and my face and peeled it off like putty. My lungs ached and I was dizzy with anoxia.

The last of my failing strength went into jerking my arm to full length. The thing flew from my hand and landed in the middle of the floor beside the curtain, making a soft cushion-like thud.

I was too weak with fright to make any further move at once; I simply lay and flooded my chest with air. There was the sound of movement: Micky sitting up, turning on a light, sliding back the curtain separating us.

"Don't get out of bed!" I cried hoarsely, rolling on one elbow.

"What is it?" Micky whispered, his face as white as mine.

*It*—the thing that had been on my face—was a lump of slowly pulsating blue jelly, translucent, veined with red, about six inches in diameter now it was humped on the floor. It seemed to flow within itself, as though searching, then began to crawl purposefully back towards my bunk. My stomach churned and I hunted for some means of driving it away.

"Micky, have you anything that will burn?" I demanded.

"Of course not—all my gear is flameproofed." He didn't take his gaze off the horrible object. "Roald, what in hell *is* that?"

Intent on disposing of both it and my lingering terror, I grabbed for my shoes. "I'll tell you when I get back," I muttered grimly. "Stay in your bunk—I don't see how it can climb a vertical slope—but don't expose bare skin to it whatever you do."

I scrambled up on the bunk and reached for the door. The catch resisted my pressure on it, and for an instant I felt another stab of terror; then I discovered that the panel was free to slide already. Someone had doctored the lock, then—but that figured, since an intruder must have brought the horrid jelly-thing. I had no time to puzzle over identities or motives. I knew what I wanted. If I could only find it . . .

At the end of the narrow corridor outside I'd noticed an emergency tool cabinet. *Let there only be a torch in it,* I thought as I sprinted towards it. And there was.

I smashed the fragmentation panel over the box's lock and seized the torch. When the startled steward—the only crewman aboard this automated ship—came to answer the alarm connected with the tool cabinet, he met me carrying a footlong sword of flame.

"Stop!" he shouted as I vanished into my own compartment, and came after me with a clatter of hard heels.

I didn't stop. I pointed the roaring torch at the jelly-thing, drunk with a primitive sense of revenge. The blob flinched from the searing flame; melted before it could do more than flinch, giving off an evil smell. The surface cauterized into scar tissue and the thing was still. The fireproof plastic of the curtain seemed more alive as it curled away from the heat.

When the whole visible surface was blackened, I withdrew the torch for a moment. A crack appeared in the covering crust and a thread of blue oozed out questingly. I conquered a desire to vomit, at least temporarily, and re-applied the flame. This time I held it on the spot till the metal floor glowed and the air was almost unbreathable with the stench. After that, there was only a charred lump like overdone meat.

For a second I stood wavering. Then I turned off the torch and thrust it into the ready hands of the steward. I pushed him out of my way and fled towards the head.

This time, I did throw up.

## 15

WHEN I felt sufficiently recovered to do so, I went back. The door of our compartment had been closed, and I had to check the reservation cards before I could tell which was the right cabin.

The air conditioners had already got rid of the odour, and Micky was trying to explain to the mystified steward. On seeing me he broke off.

"Are you all right?" he demanded anxiously.

I nodded, and apologized ridiculously to the steward, who was holding the glowing torch carefully away from his body. "If you'll just wait a moment, I'll tell you all about it."

I turned to shut the door, and found that the catch was still not operating.

"It was working all right when we came aboard," I muttered to no one in particular. I felt giddy from my narrow escape.

Going back into the corridor, I ran my fingers over the underside of the lock mechanism. As I'd expected, I touched a small disc clinging there limpet-fashion. I slid it off the edge of the lock, and the catch worked perfectly.

"Know what this is?" I asked the steward, showing him the disc.

"It's—why, it's a nullifier. Holds the wards of the lock by magnetism and stops them engaging when the door is closed."

I sat down wearily on the edge of my bunk. Guessing that I must be in a state of shock, the steward put down the torch in the corner and fumbled out a flat case from his pocket.

"Here!" he said, handing me a green tablet. "It's a euphoric—it ought to help."

I chewed on it gratefully, and it did help. Within half a minute I felt calm enough to turn to Micky and explain.

"Micky, you were asking what that lump of jelly was. It was a Sagittarian parasite. In the natural state it has the typical Sag silicon metabolism, but recently they've been building us some with a carbon base for experiments in tissue-restoration. The idea is to provide a seal for wounds which will be incorporated into the body as the incision heals. A good idea—but up to now it doesn't work. Human beings are allergic to them."

I fingered the skin of my face. So far, there was no sign of a rash, but I was certain one would erupt before we landed.

"Someone put that nullifier on the lock, crept in while we were both asleep, and put that jelly over my mouth and nose. If a miracle hadn't made me realize that I had to breathe out and not in, I'd have suffocated in complete silence. When I was found dead, there would have been no visible trace of the weapon. It would have adsorbed through the mucous membrane in my nose and united with the natural tissue."

*When I was found dead!* First the numbness of shock, now the artificial elation of the euphoric, was saving me the full force of that horror. But sooner or later I was going to have to face it.

Micky gave me a compassionate glance and turned to the steward.

"You'd better call the police and have the ship met by a lie-detector squad. Presumably they'll have to interrogate all the passengers directly we land."

"But surely they can't do that," the steward objected. "We don't know if the passengers will agree."

"Blazes!" Micky jumped to his feet. "They're going to have to put up with it! Don't you realize this is the attempted murder of a government official?"

The steward blanched. The idea of that rarest of crimes —murder—aboard his own ship obviously hadn't connected in his mind till this moment. Now he hurried out, and the door slid to with a hiss.

"Thanks," I said. "Just what I wanted to say, only I couldn't think of the right words. But—"

I hesitated.

"But what?" Micky urged.

"You're wrong," I said slowly. "Not the attempted murder of a government official."

"Roald, I don't get you. It was sure as hell intended to be murder!"

"I'm not arguing about that!" *Nor about my nearly being the victim,* I added silently. I shuddered.

"But you aren't a government official, Micky."

He exhaled sharply and his eyes became round and wide.

"Do you mean I was the one supposed to be killed? Why in the world—?"

"I'm sure of it. I didn't notice when we came aboard, but just now I had to check the reservation cards to find the right compartment. We've taken the wrong bunks. The card on this one bears your name."

"And in the dark he didn't realize. I see. But—no, just a second. He could have used black light."

"Can you see a man carrying a night-vision helmet around the ship? But he could have slipped the parasite in his pocket—it was small enough. With some sort of sealing around it to keep it from touching his skin."

There was a long silence. Watching Micky, I could almost read his mind. He was thinking: *what if the killer hadn't made a mistake? I wouldn't have guessed what was happening. I'd be lying there dead, and no one would know : . .*

To a modern man, still expecting perhaps eighty years more life, the waste entailed by premature death became not exactly more frightening—it's always been frightening —but somehow sadder than for a man able to accept that his survival was one long chain of risks passed only by chance. As a saint is said to grow more conscious of his sins as those grow fewer, so men living longer seemed more aware of their vulnerability.

Micky looked up finally and his lips quirked into a wry grin. "Shuffled off, unhousel'd, unanneal'd," he murmured. "Roald, who would have wanted to do this? And why?"

"Assuming I'm right," I parried, "who do *you* think?"

"There's one possibility that I can see, and that's so slim it's absurd. But—perhaps the Starhomers are planning the showdown I suggested, and prefer to catch Earth unawares. They might think that shutting me up would help."

"It damned well would," I muttered. I stretched my legs, realized I'd almost put my foot on the dead parasite, and drew back hastily. "How many people know about your results?"

"The computer team who processed my matrices for me may know—if they were sharp-witted enough to see the implications, which I tend to doubt."

I said thoughtfully, "I wonder if someone added two and *x* and got the right answer. In other words, I wonder if someone who wasn't sure you'd got your positive proof noticed that you were coming back to the Bureau with me, decided you must be on the right track after all, and took this panicky step to silence you."

There was another pause. Abruptly Micky said, "I think you suspect a link between the League and the Starhomers."

I almost gaped. That very idea had crossed my mind, and I was examining it to see if it was sound enough to utter.

"Well—you, and the police, and Tinescu all seemed to

believe the League would never turn from talk to action. But they have been injected with new life from somewhere. From off Earth, perhaps. Are you with me?"

Micky, chin cupped in his palm, looked like a beardless Mephistopheles as he considered the implications. Abruptly he rose in excitement.

"I've been blind! *Of course* you're right! What better way to foment distrust of BuCult and hence of Earth's ability to handle alien and colonial affairs? And the Starhomers are preparing to announce their own version of BuCult—you told me so yesterday. It fits beautifully."

"It has the extra advantage that as League ideas spread, decent, intelligent people will begin to despair of Earth's ability to look after cultural exchange. We've had League sympathizers planted in the Bureau already, haven't we?"

Micky whistled.

"Directly we land," I continued, "I think I'd better get hold of the man who's investigating these incidents where the League may be involved. Ah—" I snapped my fingers. "Inspector Klabund, that was the name."

A light tapping came at the door. We started, but when Micky slid the panel back it proved only to be the steward.

"I've called the police," he reported. "They've agreed to question all the passengers when we touch down. No one can possibly get out before we unseal the main door, so we have him trapped."

He gave a little shiver. "Unsettling, isn't it—travelling with a murderer?"

I put my hand to my face. A prickly-hot sensation was developing. Here was the rash I'd expected. Determinedly I stopped myself rubbing it and making it worse.

"How could he expect to get away with it?" the steward went on.

"He may well be registered under a false name," I said. "You see, if his plan had gone off right, no one would have suspected the means employed until they held an autopsy. By that time he could have got well away."

"Instead of which he's due for psyching," Micky said in a grim voice. "But don't let it worry you, steward. He won't try anything else. He's probably sure he succeeded, and the last thing he'll want is to draw attention on himself."

"I guess so," the steward admitted doubtfully. But he didn't seem visibly comforted as he left us with an automatic good night.

"You'd better try and catch some more sleep, Roald," Micky suggested, and I complied passively, stretching out on the bunk. To judge by the noises across the cabin, Micky had little trouble sleeping but much in finding rest. I couldn't even doze; within half an hour I gave up trying. Partly, this was because the rash on my face was burning and itching continuously now.

But much more it was due to an iron-hard, ice-cold purpose that had invaded my mind, locking on to my consciousness with bulldog fangs and promising to give me no respite till it was accomplished.

The purpose was the ending of the Stars Are For Man League.

When the express touched down, the police were waiting with grim faces. Even though their business was crime, we'd managed to make murder such a rarity that the mention of the word hung over us all like a cloud of smoke.

Quietly and competently they stopped each disembarking passenger, summarized what had happened, and led them in turn to a table on which a lie-detector had been set up. The asking of a single question sufficed to eliminate the innocent. At the seventeenth try, a white-faced man who had already been unnerved by the sight of someone he assumed to be dead standing behind the detector table made the needle of the machine jump from the true to the false side of the line.

Two burly constables moved in to flank him and stop him running away. But he attempted nothing so futile, simply let his hands fall limp to his side.

Struggling against tiredness, the aftermath of shock, and the maddening irritation on my face, I whispered to the sergeant in charge of the operation, and the latter rapped out a second query.

"Are you a member of the Stars Are For Man League?"

The man shook his head determinedly, but again the implacable needle quavered over into "false."

"Look at him!" Micky murmured to me. "Someone's got at him, and it may very well be a Starhomer. He's a Terran—he'd never be so casual about human life if he hadn't been influenced from outside."

They recorded testimony for the holding charge before they let us go, and scraped the remains of the parasite off the floor of our compartment. Organic analysis would identify not only its origin, but even the particular gene-type to which it belonged, and it shouldn't be long before they traced the murderer's source of supply.

"That man won't last ten minutes at his trial," the sergeant commented as the whimpering captive was led away. "But there's something I want to ask you, Mr Vincent. What made you mention the Stars Are For Man League? I'd always had the impression they were all talk and no action—but this is dreadful!"

"I think you'll be hearing a lot more about the League," I forced out between stiff lips. The allergy all human beings showed towards Sag parasites was bringing my hand out in tiny blisters now, as well as my face, even though I'd touched it with my fingers for only a few seconds.

The sergeant noticed my discomfort, and gestured at a constable whose lapels bore the tiny caduceus of the forensic medicine branch. He looked me over with clucks of sympathy, dug into his first-aid kit and attended to the inflammation.

"That should take care of it for the time being," he said when he had sprayed the affected areas with plastoskin. "I can give you some histaminoids to minimize the allergy, but you'll be groggy at least for the rest of the day, so don't do anything strenuous."

"Sorry," I said grimly. "I have some strenuous business to see to. Micky! Come on—Tinescu will be waiting for us."

# 16

TINESCU shut down his desk, instructing the secretary to record all his calls and tripping the switch that put the "busy" light on at the door.

"Sit down," he said, waving us to chairs. His eyes lingered on the plastoskin covering my face, which was still fresh enough to be detectable, but he didn't comment on it.

"Well, Torres? I imagine it took something galaxy-shaking to shift you from your cosy lair in Cambridge, so let me hear it. I only hope it isn't bad news."

"Depends how you look at it," Micky grunted, folding his lanky body into the chair and dumping a portfolio containing his documents on the floor at his feet. "According to my latest calculations, Starhome has finally got the edge over us and from here on out will be pulling ahead fast."

I watched Tinescu closely. I had no idea how he would take this bombshell. The last reaction I'd expected, though, was the one he showed.

All of a sudden ten years seemed to drop away from

him. For the first time I could recall he looked actually happy, and he beamed on Micky like a proud father.

"Torres, I could hug you. The waiting was driving me out of my mind."

"I was pretty sure you already knew," Micky said.

"Oh, that's putting it too strong. But you must admit it was inevitable sooner or later. Just recently there have been so many pointers I was practically biting my nails with anxiety in case we were overtaken by events. What put you wise—the nature of the survey findings which they tried to have doctored?"

"That, and a few other things."

Tinescu gave a wise nod. "They haven't neglected the soft sciences as much as we used to believe, that's definite. But since they made it a matter of policy to hide their progress from our survey missions, all we've been getting is bits and pieces. Well! This is excellent news. And perhaps," he added with a mock glare in my direction, "Roald will feel a trifle less harshly towards me for not stepping on the Starhomers' toes."

I couldn't meet his eyes; I was embarrassed. But I still had objections.

"Surely you could have raised the matter with the Minister," I suggested. "We could have made some sort of advance arrangements—"

"And told the Starhomers by implication what they didn't yet realize?" Tinescu shook his head. "Roald, I'm surprised at your lack of subtlety. Speaking of lack of subtlety, I'm sure you've deduced that it must be the Starhomers who are financing the Stars Are For Man League?"

"We reached that conclusion by another route," Micky said. "A League member tried to kill me on the way over. And got Roald by mistake."

"Is that what's made such a mess of your face?" Tinescu peered at me in great concern. "If they're getting that desperate, we shall have to—But tell me the details first."

I summarized the episode of the parasite, and Tinescu heard me out with a deepening frown.

"Well, that was an ingenious choice of weapon," he declared. "By the same token, though, it's going to make it easy to trace the person responsible. All the parasites we've had sent to Earth were gene-typed and indexed before being distributed to research labs. As a matter of fact, I've just been given the latest report on them. Care to see it?"

Thinking it was not a bad idea to learn all I could about the things which had so nearly ended my life, I put out my hand for the file he offered. It held an information copy of a communication from the Department of Pathology at Melbourne University to the Bureau's biochemical section, which stated that the university's sample Sag parasites were being returned because a certain compound—diagram of molecular structure appended—reacted on human epidermis. Please ask the Sagittarians to develop an alternative strain.

Micky twisted around to peer at the report sidewise, and demanded of Tinescu, "Where else have they been sent besides Melbourne—do you know?"

"I haven't seen the full list of recipients. But I do recall that a batch went to the Faculty of Medicine at Cambridge." He shook his head in reluctant admiration. "Using one to commit a murder! Hasn't it got a quality of diabolical genius, that?"

I didn't say anything.

"Roald!" Tinescu went on. "Who told you about these things, anyway? Because whoever it was, he saved your life. You must have had a lot of detail to realize what was happening in so short a time."

"It was like an eternity while it lasted," I muttered. "Who *did* tell me?" I pondered a moment, and then snapped my fingers. "Oh yes! Helga Micallef. Some time about the beginning of the year, when her department was having bad problems with them, she caught it from Matkyevitch—venting his frustration on the first person who came handy, the way he tends to. And she left the lab in a towering temper and the first person *she* found to share her troubles with happened to be me."

I felt a tremor of awe at the narrowness of the edge on which my life had been balanced.

"There hasn't been any reason to keep information about the things secret," Tinescu shrugged. "And I can see you're getting impatient, Torres. Sorry, go ahead."

Micky hunched forward eagerly, spreading notes all over the desk-top.

"So far Roald and I haven't had time to draw up more than a sketchy plan of action. But one thing's definite— the Starhomers will stage their showdown in not more than eighteen months from now. We shouldn't bank on longer than twelve. Now here"—selecting a sheet of closely typed figures—"is the matrix of the extreme case: letting the news break to an unprepared Earthly audience. See this set here? That's for the League and other similar organizations. It branches in about six directions, all bad; the best we can hope for is a strong lobby at governmental level in favour of imposing an economic boycott on Starhome."

"The best?" echoed Tinescu in dismay.

Micky gave a sour chuckle. "You should see the bad extra-polations! Now here's the set which defines our advantage—I've assigned it a minimum value, one year flat. We know for sure, and the Starhomers are only guessing, that the balance point is past. We've got to exploit that for all it's worth. The budget will run to about six and a half billion for propaganda alone, and half will have to go at governmental level."

"As much as half?" Tinescu snapped.

"Easily. The first thing—see the line which develops at the bottom?—the first thing the Starhomers will do when they realise their strength is demand the abrogation of their colonial contracts with us, and they won't like it if we put up too fierce a resistance."

"I'd better start working on the Minister right away," Tinescu muttered.

"Don't forget we have to deal with the popular audience too. Newscasts, mass education—that sort of thing. We've got to convince the people that we'll still be on the same planet."

"How about Starhome?" I interjected. "We've got to persuade them that just because they get their own way in this doesn't mean everything will be roses from now on."

"I was coming to that," Micky nodded. "The longest part of the job is to make up Starhome's deficiencies in the human sciences. It may take fifty years. Fortunately they already realize the need for it. Did Roald tell you they're going to set up their own counterpart of BuCult?"

Tinescu's eyes blazed at me. "No, he did not!"

"I'm sorry, chief," I excused myself. "I only heard about this on Friday afternoon when the Starhomer courier called on me. You'd gone—it was after sixteen by then."

"What's she got to do with it? Oh, never mind—it was to be expected, I guess. Go on," he rapped at Micky.

After that I thought it better to keep my mouth shut. My comments would have been superfluous anyway. At the end of an hour I was marvelling all over again at the range and scope of Micky's mind. Subject to a computer check in Integration, one might almost have said the plan was polished and ready to roll.

But it only seemed that easy. Public opinion possesses appalling inertia, and we were barred from using the crude mass-appeal phenomena like sabotaging rockets which the Starhomers didn't hesitate to employ.

Still . . . if anyone could swing the deal, Micky Torres could. I gave him a crooked grin.

"How does it feel to be the most important man on Earth?" I asked.

He pulled a face at me and didn't answer.

Finally the moment came when Tinescu reached for the phone and called Tomas in Integration to tell him that a crash priority job was coming down and that he should clear current programmes but not feed in any more until Micky arrived. There was a yelp of complaint, but Tinescu swore at him in Rumanian and that persuaded him.

"Now, what about you, Roald?" the old man demanded.

I stumbletongued for a second. "Well—I'm going to see Klabund, I guess. He's in by far the best position to tackle the League—he has three inquiries in hand with which they may be connected, and all of them are *sub judice* so there's no risk of the information being made public knowledge for some time yet."

"You want to tip him off about the link between Starhome and the League—yes?"

I nodded.

"Think he should, Torres?"

Micky considered it for a moment, and finally said, "Yes, I think it's a sensible move. Provided that at all costs we don't let the Starhomers know we were the people who spotted the connection. Let them believe they were clumsy enough to allow a dumb policeman to catch on. Then they'll have to pick another line of attack, and we'll gain some room to manœuvre."

He shook all his documents together in a neat pile and headed for Integration to launch the biggest mass education campaign ever undertaken by mankind.

## 17

EXACTLY why a narrow escape from death and the prospect of becoming a citizen of a second-class planet should have made me feel I was enjoying myself, I couldn't figure out. But I was. Something was taking hold of me—a sense of purpose, one might have called it, which promised challenges deeper and more rewarding than any work I'd tackled in BuCult since I joined it. One of the first effects was that I felt I was getting my priorities straight. The sight of the mound of work that had accumulated in the conveyor box over the week-end would normally have made me sigh and sit down to sift painstakingly through every item before initiating fresh tasks. Now I ignored it and reached for the phone.

My secretary started to recite a list of work on hand. I shut it off.

"How can I contact Inspector Klabund, Pacific Coast Police District?" I demanded of the exchange.

"An attempt will be made to locate him for you," said the horrible sweet mechanical voice at the other end.

I waited. At length: "Inspector Klabund is unavailable at police headquarters. The inquiry into the recent rocket-crash is in progress and he is believed to be conducting an investigation at the port. If you wish to record a message—"

*Begin speaking after the third tone.* I scowled at the blank screen over the phone. "Find out when he'll be available. I want a personal appointment with him."

Another pause. Fortunately Klabund had remembered to

key that information into his own secretary. He would be back, I was told, at fourteen hours.

"Record, please . . . Inspector Klabund, Roald Vincent of BuCult will call on you at fourteen today with important new information concerning your current inquiries."

I switched off and sat back. Now: Patricia. The small matter of my nearly being murdered had made me forget to call her from the rocketport when I got back. I was forgetting to call her so easily that I was becoming worried.

I told the phone to connect me with Area Met, not really expecting her to accept the call. While waiting, I wondered how I could track her down—go round to her place this evening, maybe . . .

"Why, Roald! Oh, I'm so glad you aren't angry with me!"

And there she was: sleek golden hair, ripe luscious mouth, dancing eyes, framed like an artist's miniature in the tiny screen of the phone. For long seconds I just gazed at her, feeling all over again the twisting sensation her beauty had first aroused in me. Then I said, "Angry?"

"I thought you must be, and that was why I hadn't heard from you."

"There was a little matter of an answerer which had instructions to refuse my calls," I hinted.

Crestfallen, she nodded. "That was a dreadful thing to do, wasn't it? But you see . . . well, I'd begun to think that we were going to stay together for a long time, and when you made that joke at the Dembas' party, about going off for goodness knows how long to Regulus, I was—well—sort of shaken."

It was my turn to be shaken. I'd never imagined that she was thinking, like me, that our relationship would last indefinitely. I felt a warm glow inside.

"Will you forgive and forget?" she pleaded.

"You know damned well I could forgive you practically anything," I said.

"And you're not angry?"

"Of course not."

"I'm so glad!" Her smile lit up her face like a nova. "I cancelled that silly order to the phone long ago, and still you didn't try to get in touch—What happened?"

"A good many things. Mainly, I was in Cambridge seeing Micky Torres. Also someone nearly killed me on the way home."

"What? Darling, you aren't serious!"

"No?" I touched my face gingerly. "It doesn't show on the phone, but I'm covered in plastoskin." I summed up the eventful journey home.

"Oh, how awful!" Eyes wide, she leaned close to the camera at her end. "Look, you must come around tonight —I'll make dinner for you and you can have a nice quiet evening. Shall we say nineteen-thirty?"

I would say nineteen-thirty. I did. And rang off with the impression I was on top of the world.

I basked for a good ten minutes before realizing that whatever else might have happened I still had a job to do here, and turned with resignation to the pile of work in the conveyor box.

Most of it had to be flagged for holding, since by now Micky's team would be monopolizing the facilities of Integration; I returned seven files of social assay data from Viridis without a pang to the central registry. But there was some processed material to be farmed out to places as close to home as Montreal or as far away as Auckland, New Zealand.

I'd just checked the time and found to my surprise that it lacked only ten minutes to the noon recess, when the annunciator of the door spoke up.

"Vincent? Martin van 't Hoff here. Can you spare a minute?"

Madeleine's spacecrew cousin. Yes, why not? I tripped the door release and the familiar red-clad figure came in.

"Hope I'm not disturbing you," he said, holding out his hand. "I was just saying good-bye to Jacky, and he mentioned your office was next door, so I thought I'd have a word while I was here."

"Congratulations," I said. "You've been promoted."

He glanced down self-consciously at the newly brilliant badge of a master navigator which had replaced the former, smaller one of a navigator-in-ordinary. "Yes—thanks. Actually that's why I'm leaving. The news came through on Saturday, and with it a posting to a new ship. I'm due to lift tonight on the Viridis run. What's more I hear we'll be carrying some of your people."

"That's right—staff from the survey missions who've been home on furlough. Oh! You must be with the *Mizar,* then. I seemed to recall she was due out today."

"Correct," he said, pleased. "Jacky said you have some friends on Viridis—any messages?"

"You might say hullo to Wlaclaw Soong. He's the port liaison officer at Viridis Main. We were in school together."

"Will do." He reached in one of his capacious pockets and found a notepad already inscribed with a long list of names. "Frankly," he muttered as he added the new one, "I'm beginning to worry about my cousin's morals. So far she's told me to give her love to thirty-one people on Viridis. Still, so long as they stay at a distance I guess Jacky needn't worry."

He tucked the notepad back in its place. "Oh, by the way, wasn't it you I was talking to about the *Algenib* when that Regulan arrived at the party?"

"That's right." I could tell he was fidgeting, even though he wanted to talk; I deduced he might be in a hurry and got up. "Look, I'm due for lunch in five minutes anyway—shall I come down to the lobby with you if you're short of time?"

"That's very kind of you—I am in a bit of a rush."

I told my secretary I was leaving, and ordered a car for

thirteen-fifteen hours to take me to see Klabund; then we headed for the elevators. Waiting for the car to arrive, I reminded Martin of what he'd been saying.

"Oh yes. I'd just thought of something when Anovel came in, and I've been back to the port to see if I'd guessed right. They'd humped the ship to her berth, and what with the lugger still in the way and the Starhomers being secretive all over the place I didn't get a very good view. No one's being allowed on board, apparently—they even have their own maintenance crew with them."

The elevator arrived and we stepped inside.

"But," Martin went on, "I did pick up some hints which seem to confirm my theory. What's different about the *Algenib* is the design of the engine holds. I think I told you why it's necessary to carry five or six engines—yes? Well, I can't for the life of me see how you could fit more than two engines into the space available."

"You mean they've found out how to reduce the size of a stardrive motor?" I hazarded, for he was looking at me as though I ought to be immensely impressed. The elevator came to a halt, and we went into the lobby.

"Well—no, not without inventing an entirely new form of propulsion. Tolerances are already down to monomolecular levels, and there's a fixed lower limit on the size of the field which will shift the *Algenib's* mass. She must weigh every ounce of fourteen thousand tons."

"Fifteen," I said.

"Really?" He pursed his lips. "Well, that settles it. They've discovered how to cancel the orbital distortions induced by the field. In other words, they can re-use their stardrive engines."

That meant very little to me, and my face must have shown the fact, for Martin went on fiercely, "Have you *no* idea what this means? Blazes, I'm not an engineer, but for the exams I took to get my master's certificate, I had to dig pretty deep into stardrive theory. The field permanently collapses the orbits of electrons at the focus of the generator—or up till now it was 'permanently'. But if they've found out how to cancel that, the Starhomers must be on to counter-gravity, to start with! Soon they'll be building ships that don't need jets for landing but float down, like balloons! Conversely, they ought to be able to produce condensed matter—nucleonium, the stuff you find in the heart of a dwarf star. Since it isn't the mass you're shifting that really counts in a starship, but the radius of the nullity field you have to generate, think how much cargo they'll be able to carry. As far as I can see they've opened up a whole new domain of physics!"

By this time we had paused on the steps of the entrance to the Bureau, with the huge motto overhead. I was silent for half a minute under Martin's quizzical gaze.

"It is disturbing, isn't it?" he said at last. "When I think I may live to fly in a ship that lifts from a planet like a bit of thistledown, and goes into hyperphotonic drive as soon as it leaves atmosphere, my guts turn over with excitement . . . Well, I really have to run. There's my car waiting. Good-bye—hope to see you when I'm next on Earth."

He ran to the car which stood, gleaming the same red as his uniform, at the foot of the steps. I watched him go, my mind churning with the impact of what he'd told me.

I was still there, numbed, when a hand fell on my shoulder and Jacky spoke from behind me.

"Roald, you look as if you've been struck by lightning!"

I shook myself and came back to the present. "Oh, hullo. Are you lunching at the canteen?"

"Naturally. The date I kept for you with Patricia exhausted my eating-out allowance for this month. I'm not like you wealthy bachelors—I have a wife and child to support." His handsome dark face was alive with amusement.

I did my best to produce an answering smile and together we crossed the street to the annexe housing the

Bureau's canteen and staff residential quarters. Strictly we should have used the underground tunnel connecting the two buildings, but traffic was light around here except in the mornings and evenings, and anyhow it was a fine warm day.

As we settled to a table, and Jacky gave a piercing whistle to attract the robot waiter, I said, "Jacky, I've just been talking to Martin van 't Hoff."

"Hm? Oh yes. He said he was going to look in on you."

"Did he mention to you this Starhomer ship which brought the Tau Cetians here—the *Algenib*?"

Jacky's face suddenly grew strained. He covered his tension by an over-careful scrutiny of the menu which the waiter flashed on its little screen.

"Yes, he's full of it at the moment. He has some vague theories about a design break-through they've made out there."

"The theories didn't seem at all vague to me," I persisted.

He stabbed angrily at buttons on the waiter, selecting his food, and it wheeled silently over to my side of the table, where it went on waiting until I forced Jacky to speak.

At long last he said, "Damn you, Roald. Do you have to rub my nose in it?"

Horrified, I took in the point which sheer obtuseness had prevented me from seeing earlier: that if the colonists had really made such an immense stride forward, Jacky was going to carry the can for the failure of the survey missions to send us advance warning. He was responsible for handling all technical data from the human colonies, as I was for all cultural and social material.

"Jacky, I'm sorry!" I exclaimed.

He sighed. "No, I'm the one who should apologize. I have no business snapping at you when I'm really angry at the Starhomers. Aren't you going to eat anything?"

I started, and chose my meal hastily, almost at random, so allowing the waiter to roll away.

"Who's the head of technical analysis out at Starhome?" I said. "And what's he been doing lately, that such a big news item escaped the missions completely?"

"He picked up a virus and went on sick leave, and I don't know the guy who's been left in charge. Some greenhorn . . . That's why I'm sore at the comptroller who named him—Charisse Wasawati. Yet I'd have staked my reputation on her as one of the ablest people we have." He ran his fingers through his crisp curly hair. "Roald, I get the impression these Starhomers have been playing us like fish —giving us what they wanted us to know, and keeping secrets we damned well ought to have dug out long ago!"

For a moment I was tempted to tell him Micky's view: that we'd passed the point at which Starhome became the leading human planet. But I didn't; the material was still in the computers, and once it had been checked out, everyone in the Bureau would have to be informed officially.

With a great air of changing the subject, he began to talk rapidly about a new Viridian symphonic poem he'd just heard, and I fell in with his conversation as best I could. But when we returned to the Bureau at ten past thirteen we both knew neither of us had been interested in what the other was saying.

## 18

IN leaving at thirteen-fifteen I was cutting it fine—Pacific Coast District police headquarters was sixty miles from here. I told the car to follow the expressway route and get ahead of schedule in the hundred-fifty lane; then I leaned back in the cushioned seat and mentally mapped what I wanted to say to Klabund.

I was going to have to allow for the after-effects of our first meeting. Tinescu had inveigled him into a breach of police ethics with that portable lie-detector, and he wouldn't have been human if my catching him out didn't rankle. So he would have a reflex tendency to discount anything I said—especially since I was bringing only a chain of tenuous suspicions, not concrete court-of-law evidence.

How could I make it sound convincing, and at the same time persuade him that he must take no action before the Bureau told him to? I decided the best course was to be absolutely factual and sober—especially, I'd have to refrain from appearing angry at my escape from death, in case he thought I was exaggerating as a compensation for the shock.

I reached my destination three minutes ahead of time. Klabund was already in his office and I was shown directly to it. He was listening to a newscast as I entered; the announcer was reporting the latest adjournment of the rocket crash inquiry, and his voice was indignant.

He greeted me politely and waved me to a chair.

"I understand you want to see me in connection with the attempt on your life which was made this morning," he suggested.

Only this morning? Days seemed to have gone by since then. I nodded.

"Do you mind if I record this?" he continued, hand hovering over a switch on his desk.

"It'll have to go under seal, I'm afraid—but I'll consent to recording provided you scramble it."

The newscast gave way to the regular pre-hourly bulletin from Area Met; he shut it off and with a sigh activated the scrambler on his recorder.

"Go ahead," he invited.

I put my hand up absently to the slick dressing on my face. "The attempt on *my* life," I said. "I don't think I was the intended victim. I think my companion was the target —we'd accidentally exchanged bunks on coming aboard."

Klabund gave a wary nod. "And your companion was—?"

"Micky Torres. You may have heard of him."

"Is that Miguel Torres, who wrote *Stars Beckoned?*"

"That's the man. Primarily he's not a writer, but our leading authority on Starhomer social evolution. He was on his way to the Bureau to make an extremely important report concerning Starhome, and we think an attempt was made to silence him—out of panic.

"We also think there is definite indication of a link between the Stars Are For Man League and the Starhomers."

Klabund turned that over in his mind. Finally he said, "It fits. You'll have to be more specific, but one of the dead ends we've run into on this inquiry is the question of what's made the League become a menace instead of a fanatical talking-shop. Neither their new finances nor the complete change of tactics can be traced to Earthside origins."

He cocked his head, waiting for me to substantiate the theory.

"We don't yet know *why* the Starhomers want to encourage the League," I admitted at once. "Our strongest suspicion is this. On Friday I learned that they plan to found a rival organization to BuCult—as I'm sure you know, that area is where they lag most markedly behind ourselves. We feel they may be trying to cast doubt on Earth's ability to deal with alien contact, to excite sympathy for their claim for a chance to tackle the problem."

"If that's your opinion, I suppose I must respect you as experts in the field," he muttered dubiously. "But it seems very thin . . . I don't imagine you can tell me the nature of this important disclosure Torres was due to make?"

"I'm very sorry, I can't. We're testing it in our computers, and till the job's done I mustn't talk about it."

He shrugged. "Assuming you're right, anyhow: who could have known about it and been sufficiently alarmed to try and—I think you said 'silence him'?"

"The computer team in Cambridge who processed his data for him. There is, incidentally, a chapter of the League there."

"I'll follow it up, certainly. It's no worse than some of our other leads. But I can make no promises, you understand?"

I nodded. "Looking for Starhomer influence on the League ought to be fairly simple, though," I suggested.

"Not really. Starhomers enjoy the same rights as Earthly natives. We don't make special provisions to trace their comings and goings." Klabund chewed his lower lip. "But thanks anyway for coming to see me. Oh, by the way, I was going to ask your chief something—I might as well ask you since you're here. This isn't confidential." He shut off the scrambler.

"You remember Dr bin Ishmael received a threat from some anonymous source about what the League would do to his visiting aliens if they were allowed to roam about?"

"Yes, he told me."

"We're assuming that the damage done to the airpipe on the Tau Cetians' quarters was their way of implementing the threat. Dr bin Ishmael says it can't have been coincidence that the race which was attacked was the one your Bureau has most trouble with. I'd be inclined to agree, except that I can't trace any information leak which would have enabled the League to tell where the delegation was accommodated. Is it possible that the knowledge was available to personnel at the Bureau?"

"It certainly wasn't on our Tau Cetian master file. I'd

read that the morning of their arrival." I frowned. Some-where at the back of memory Klabund's words had started an itch, but nothing would come clear. I continued slowly, "I guess it could have been passed on casually, but it's very much a Bureau habit to leave work at the office, so it's unlikely to have been made public through conversation with outsiders."

"I see." Klabund pushed back his chair. "Well, we shall just have to keep on digging till we trace the leak—if there was one."

It was an obvious hint for me to leave him, and I did so willingly enough; I'd said all I wanted to.

None the less, for the rest of the day I couldn't concentrate on my Bureau work. That last question of Klabund's ran-kled. It did seem unlikely that of the five races represented at the Ark the one singled out for attack should be the latest to be contacted, the most difficult to deal with, and the one whose metabolism had been least thoroughly inves-tigated—so that they were most likely to be killed outright, our surgeons and doctors helpless to heal them.

Since it had happened, then, the implication was the killer had known what he was after. He knew, in short, that in G Block were the Tau Cetians.

Odd. Very odd. You'd expect a random attack to be made from the public road passing the Ark. But G Block was at the back of the site . . .

Something there? I grabbed at the elusive recollection, and slippery as an eel it eluded me again. I shook my head and reached to answer an incoming call.

It was the Professor of Modern Anglic Literature from Montreal University. I spent ten minutes talking fast to persuade him that his analysis of recent Viridian drama not only could wait but was going to—like everything else due for processing by Integration it had been postponed to make way for Micky's vital task—and then another five explaining why without once defining the actual reason. I was rather proud of myself; the professor rang off with a misty but distinct impression that he had been honoured with a glimpse of the workings of government which his duty as a citizen prevented him from letting go any further.

Sixteen-thirty came without my having trapped the maddening mental flea Klabund's question had started jumping around my skull. I packed up and headed for home.

My face was no longer sore. I took the risk of peeling off the plastoskin, and was delighted to find that it had done its work already; the eruption of blisters had been stopped before it was really serious, and the skin was pinkly clean and soft. My hand, too, was healing fast.

Eager to see Patricia, I hurried through a bath and a change of clothes—so quickly, I allowed too much time, and when I arrived at her apartment had to waste five minutes walking up and down the street. I knew how much trouble she would go to over the dinner she was preparing; to be called to the door ahead of schedule might spoil some crucial stage of the sauce, I feared.

One minute past the due time, I was at her door. She came out to meet me in a backless halter and skin-tight pants of a lime-green so pale it looked white in the brilliance of the corridor lighting.

"Darling! Are you all right?" she exclaimed, worriedly inspecting my face.

"Marvellous," I said.

"That's my line!" She kissed me firmly and drew me inside. "Oh, Roald, I'm so glad all the fuss and bother is over!"

"It doesn't look that way to me," I commented as I glanced around the apartment. The arrangements were impressive; she'd put colour-filters on the lights, which made her clothes a shifting pattern of changing tints as she moved about, and the air was full of mouth-watering scents.

"Silly!" But she was pleased at my reaction. "That's not what I meant. I don't think of it as 'fuss and bother' to make you welcome."

"Judging by the way you're dressed," I said, "you had more than a polite hello in mind."

She looked down at herself. "Don't you like it?" she demanded. "I bought this outfit specially."

"*Like it?* It's very nearly as eye-popping as you are."

"Roald, you're sweet." She hugged me, then drew back at arm's length to stare up into my face with a trace of anxiety.

"You have, really, forgiven me, haven't you?"

I showed her.

"Mm-*hm*!" she forced out at last. "You've made a quick recovery. Here I was expecting an invalid, and . . . ! Sit down; I'll fix you a drink. And in exactly eleven minutes it'll be time for dinner."

It ought to have been a flawless evening—a flawless *night*. Usually I was the one desperate to please her, afraid of offending her, of driving her away. Tonight she was going to unprecedented lengths to please me—the food was magnificent, the wine and the liqueurs that followed so expensive I was taken aback. And when I over-ruled her laughing protests about my being supposed to take things gently because of my dreadful experience on the way home from England, she let herself go with a passion and violence I'd never known before.

Yet when she had sunk into an exhausted slumber, snuggled close beside me in her huge soft bed, two ridiculous nagging ideas kept my own eyes open a while longer.

The first was perhaps rooted in what Tinescu had defined for me—the suggestion that I didn't have as much confidence in myself as other people did. I was paradoxically disturbed by the thought that she was altogether *too* eager to please me.

*Stupid!* I rebuked myself.

But I couldn't dismiss the second problem so lightly, though it was equally minor. At the instant before the last climax, I'd found myself wondering what it would be like if this weren't Patricia, but Kay.

I stared down at her lovely tousled hair for a long while, thinking that I ought to know more about her than I did. I knew she was an orphan; I knew she didn't like talking about the loss of her parents, so I'd never questioned her closely. Some time I should—some time . . .

I drowsed off.

During the night I had a fearful dream. I imagined that Patricia was leaning over me as I lay on my back, kissing me hungrily, and that her face became soft, and spread, and oozed all over mine like the Sag parasite, blocking my nostrils with a horrid slick jelly until I suffocated.

It was so terrible that I came awake moaning, and half-aroused her. She threw her arm over me and murmured my name, and I went gratefully back to darkness.

## 19

AFTERNOON sunlight reached yellow fingers through the windows of the courtroom, touching the polished brass pans of the symbolic scales on the judge's desk and lying in bright pools at the feet of the assembled witnesses. There were only four of us: Micky, who was unconcernedly reading a file of social assay documents, the steward of the express, the police sergeant whose lie-detector squad had met us at the port on landing, and myself.

I wasn't looking forward to the next hour or so. I'd never been to a sanity trial before—though of course like everyone else I'd been taught about modern judicial procedure in school—and I certainly had never thought this was how I'd attend my first one.

The public gallery was half empty. That surprised me at first, in view of the sensational nature of the charge; then I reflected that maybe nowadays we'd become civilized enough to resist the morbid temptation to come and gloat over a man's destruction. Psyching wasn't cruel, but it was far from kind, and in this case it was the only possible verdict.

I noted a palely pretty woman in the front row of the public seats, whose hands never stopped twisting a handkerchief back and forth. I wondered if she was the wife, or sister, or girl friend of the accused man.

His name had proved to be Hugues Castle, and his job, so I was informed, was that of full-time organizer and publicist for the Cambridge chapter of the League. That was another new development—a year ago, funds wouldn't have stretched to anything but volunteer labour.

He had just been brought in, and now sat facing the judge's table with his advocate on one side and a policeman on the other. Meantime, the clerk of the court and a government inspector were checking the operation of the lie-detector at the side of the witness chair. Finally the inspector thumb-printed the seal of approval to show the machine was working in accordance with legal requirements, and there was a moment of tense expectancy.

During it, I realized with some shame that like most people I didn't have the faintest idea how lie-detectors worked—I took them as much for granted as cars or phones. I was about to lean towards Micky, when the door of the judge's chambers slid back and we had to rise.

The judge was a woman of late middle age—about seventy-five—in the university gown of a doctor of criminal sociology. She took her place, nodded for us to resume our seats, and picked up a written questionnaire which summarized the direction of the whole trial.

"This is the case of the Human Race versus one Hugues Castle," she said briskly. "Is the accused present?"

A shiver ran down my back. That was a terrifying notion —the Human Race against one man!

The clerk stood up. "He is present," he agreed.

"Read the charge."

"The charge is," the clerk said, turning to face Castle, "that you, Hugues Castle, being at the time a passenger aboard trans-Atlantic express rocket liner serial number 191905, did at or about one hour fifteen minutes on the fourth day of March this year place an organism from the third planet of Sigma Sagittarii, namely a mutated pseudamoeboid Dockeri, over the mouth and nose of one Roald Savage Vincent, an employee of the Bureau of Cultural Relations, well knowing that such action could result in death."

There followed playbacks of the evidence which I, Micky and the steward had recorded on arriving at the rocketport; each of us in turn was called before the lie-detector to certify that this was a true recording. The police sergeant confirmed having taken these depositions, then went on to describe how he had screened the passengers of the express and discovered that Castle was the culprit. He spoke in a clear, rather monotonous voice, and throughout the needle of the lie-detector never wavered past the line dividing truth from falsehood.

That established the deed as a fact. There remained the question of whether the accused had consciously intended murder. As the clerk led Castle to the witness chair, the judge interrupted for the first time.

"Donald!"

"Yes, Mrs Gladshaw?" the clerk said, turning.

"Give this to the defence advocate, will you?" She held out a folded document. "The police have asked me to put some additional questions not covered in the preliminary hearings—I believe they're in order, but I'd like advocate's assent."

A buzz of surprise went around the court. Glancing towards the public seats again, I saw the pale woman was now using her handkerchief to weep into. Definitely a relation or lover of Castle's—at a pinch, she might even be his mother, for weeping made her look much older.

The advocate rose and gave back the document. His was a thankless task in such a case, I imagined; all he could do was advance mitigating circumstances.

"Defence agrees that these questions are in order!"

"Thank you. Now, Mr Castle . . ."

With unfailing politeness the judge posed the damning questions; Castle answered in a thin strained voice. Yes, it was reasonable to expect that the parasite would block the nostrils and mouth; yes, a man who couldn't breathe would die; yes, he'd been aware of all this at the time in question.

I couldn't hate him for what he'd done. He was more an object of pity, to my mind. Anyone whose mental horizons were so shrunken and deformed as his must be a miserable half-person.

And suddenly the judge asked, "Did you mean to kill Roald Vincent?"

The audience assumed an affirmative. Instead, Castle uttered a resigned, "No!"

The lie-detector stayed on the "true" side. There was a murmur of bewilderment.

"Did you in fact plan to make Miguel Torres the victim?

You can see the man I mean in the witnesses' row, next to the police sergeant."

Castle didn't look round. He merely muttered, "Yes . . ."

The defence advocate rose. "I'd respectfully remind the court that at this point the questions overlap with a public inquiry material germane to which is *sub judice*," he said.

"Thank you," the judge murmured. "I have no intention of pursuing this line further."

I noticed that Micky was paying full attention for the first time. The reason was obvious; he didn't want the Starhomers to get wind of our discovery that they were connected with the League until he felt the moment was ripe. But what had been said seemed to satisfy him, and he went back to his reading.

The defence advocate rose now and did his best; he painted a grim picture of an unhappy childhood and persecution by an unkind society. It was scarcely convincing, but it had to be taken into account by the court before sentence was passed.

The judge listened intently to every word. The public didn't, and I could guess what was distracting them. Not once in the whole proceedings had the question come up of *why* Castle wanted to commit this murder.

I hoped no inspired guesswork would reveal the truth.

Finally the judge addressed Castle with the same politeness as throughout the afternoon.

"Mr Castle, we hereby find that you did the act of which you are accused. We also find that you knew the probable consequences, and you likewise knew that doing something to bring about a man's death is a crime known as murder, the penalties for which are public knowledge. In accordance with modern criminal codes, a person who does what you have done is regarded as insane, and for the safeguarding of society a course of action is prescribed from which I am not empowered to depart.

"At any time in the next fifteen days you may appeal against the conduct of this trial; you may submit all or any part of the evidence to computer scrutiny and try to show that the cause of justice has not been properly served. Failing that, this court decrees that you shall be submitted to a form of psychotherapy that shall in the opinion of a qualified orthopsychic practitioner render you incapable of again committing a crime."

She pushed back her chair.

"The court is closed. Good afternoon to you all."

And the pale woman in the front row of the public seats slid to the floor in a dead faint.

"Your Inspector Klabund is a very subtle man," Micky said as we left the courthouse.

"And the defence advocate must have been pretty ready to co-operate," I said.

"Yes. I was wondering how they'd keep the League out of the evidence. But then of course I realized that it would follow automatically—they were only putting one man on trial, not an organization or a creed. A modern trial is really marvellously simple, isn't it?"

"It'd be a hell of a sight simpler," I countered sourly, "if human beings weren't so complicated."

He chuckled. "We've wanted absolute justice for about ten thousand years. Short of mind-reading, nothing will make the law much faster or more accurate than it is today. I can't think of any way to improve it."

"If *you* can't, I won't bother to try. Speaking of mind-reading, though, I realized while we were in there that I haven't the slightest idea how a lie-detector works. I have this foggy notion, left over from when I was a kid, that it's some sort of mechanical telepathy. And since we've been basing our legal system on it for about a century now, I think I ought to straighten myself out.

"Telepathy it certainly *doesn't* use! Let me see—there was a girl I knew at Cambridge, reading criminal sociology, and she told me about lie-detectors ... Oh yes. They measure the degree of congruence between the recollection and the utterance. It takes a certain additional effort to tell a lie. Of course they aren't foolproof—one may be honestly mistaken, or under a post-hypnotic command. But modern psychology can decide whether a witness actually knows what he's talking about before he's called into court."

He cocked his head. "Better than it was in the old days, Roald! There was a time when just about every statute on the books had another to contradict it, in some other country or even in the same country. Read up on it some time and you'll see how lucky we are. Going back to the Bureau?"

I checked my watch. "Yes, I guess so—I can fit in a little work before quitting time."

## 20

ON reaching my office, however, I didn't tackle my work at once. Instead, I called the Ark to inquire after the Tau Cetians. I couldn't locate bin Ishmael, but I did speak to Gobind, the lab chief. Despite the black rings under his eyes testifying to the pressure under which he was still working, he sounded happy.

"All but one of the five are back on their feet now. Dr bin Ishmael thinks we've sold them on the story of an accident due to negligence, and Shvast hasn't said anything to indicate they think we're deceiving them. Matter of fact, we intend to stage a little drama for them this evening—this atmosphere engineer who's due for posting away will be 'fired' under circumstances of maximum humiliation. Vroazh wanted to punish him rather barbarically, but Shvast argued that this might lower their degree of civilization in our eyes, and won him around to accepting our proposals. I don't think we'll have any more trouble with them."

"Fine!" I exclaimed in relief, and would have rung off but that he gestured for me to wait a moment.

"Look, is there any way we can have the police taken off our backs?"

"I don't quite understand," I said.

"Place is crawling with them. Something to do with this hybrid three-legged inquiry Klabund is running. They're interviewing everyone who knew the Tau Cetians were housed in G Block, and the time they're using up is appalling! Couldn't I get someone at the Bureau to drop some heavy hints? Who should I ask?"

"It'll have to be Tinescu," I said. "Or you could try Indowegiatuk, I guess."

"She's on the side of the police. Cantankerous old baggage . . . Well, thanks anyway. Maybe I will try Tinescu."

His image faded. I reached for a waiting file. But I couldn't concentrate on it. Once again something was irking the back of my mind—not the same thing which Klabund's question had set skipping about my skull like a flea yesterday, but something else perhaps even more important.

Determined this time to get to the bottom of it, I shut my eyes and leaned back, marshalling a whole bunch of factors. Starhomer technical superiority . . . Martin van 't Hoff . . . the *Algenib* . . . the Tau Cetians . . . Kay . . .

No, that was taking it too far. I backtracked.

And suddenly I had it.

I sat bolt upright on my chair, my eyes wide open but taking in nothing. It was fantastic, but my rudimentary technical knowledge didn't allow me to say it was impossible. Maybe it was better so—someone with proper technical training might have dismissed it out of hand.

I reached to the phone. "Get me Inspector Klabund!" I exclaimed. "Priority!"

Fortunately he was in his office. Unfortunately he didn't want to be interrupted: the screen reddened as the secretary-to-record circuit was overridden by my priority demand.

He scowled at me from the screen. "What is it, Mr Vincent? I'm up to my eyes at the moment!"

"I've had an inspiration," I said. "You have the section of airpipe which was damaged in the attack on the Tau Cetians?"

"Of course, it's in our labs right now."

"I want you to go over the face of the pipe which was farthest from the wall. I think you'll find another hole in it directly opposite the larger one."

Klabund looked openly annoyed. "Mr Vincent, there isn't such a hole! We'd have noticed it. I ordered it to be examined and it was examined—I've seen the report myself, and there's only the one hole."

"Did they go over the pipe with a microscope?"

"Looking for holes? Why in the world should they? A three-inch tear is big enough to do all the damage we have to account for!"

I shook my head. "Tell your forensic people to look again—this time, for a hole so small the naked eye doesn't notice it."

"And if it's there, what will it prove?" Klabund snapped.

"It will be the hole left by the projectile which tore open the pipe. A bullet, presumably."

Klabund took a deep breath. "Mr Vincent, I don't know how busy you are. Myself, I'm conducting an extensive and *very* complicated inquiry, and I have people screaming down my neck for quick results. Do you mind getting the hell off this phone?"

I hesitated, long enough to check on two facts in my mind's eye: first, of course, whether I was confident of what I was saying. I decided I was.

Second, I ran through two little tables of rank-structure. Klabund's went: inspector—superintendent—commissioner—Minister of Justice. Mine went: assistant —Chief of Bureau—Minister of Extra-Terrestrial Affairs. We were both government employees; I was one step nearer the top.

I said, "All right, do it your way. Inspector Klabund, I rank you. I order you to examine that pipe for such a hole as I have described."

I'd never seen such a raw fury in a man's face before. He broke the connection with a gesture like a sword-thrust, and I immediately began to have second thoughts. It was too late to worry now, of course—the conversation would have been recorded, and if I proved to have pulled rank without good cause and wasted his valuable time, the least I could expect was a severe reprimand.

For the next fifteen minutes I was in an agony of suspense. I welcomed the buzz of the phone when it next came. Perhaps, I thought, Patricia was calling—she'd told me she was flying up to Alaska tonight to see her married sister, and she'd promised to say good-bye before leaving for the rocketport.

But it wasn't her. It was Klabund again, and so subdued I felt an enormous sinking weight of relief.

"I owe you an apology," he said without preamble. "I sent down to the lab, and they found the hole at once. It isn't even microscopic—it's about point zero five of an inch across. Some blockhead decided it wasn't worth looking at closely because it was so small! Now they have examined it, though, it turns out to look exactly like a miniature bullet-hole. How in the *galaxy* did you know it had to be there?"

I conquered my jubilation and remembered to ask him to turn on his scrambler.

"I don't think they can be blamed, inspector," I said. "They were looking for something to make an exit hole three inches across, weren't they? And since they'd ruled out explosives or atomics, they'd also ruled out a connection with this tiny hole."

"But I thought you said this was made by the projectile! In that case, we're going to have to bring atomics back into consideration—"

"No, you won't," I launched my own bombshell with some pride. "It was a bullet of condensed matter."

"Mr Vincent, I thought you were on the social assay side, not the technical side. I've heard of condensed matter as a theoretical possibility, but I didn't know it had been made yet."

"Hear me out. You know it was a ship built at Starhome which brought the Tau Cetians here? Well, I've been told unofficially"—a fine way of dressing-up Martin van 't Hoff's guesswork, I glossed mentally—"that the design breakthrough which that ship represents implies a means of directly manipulating electron orbits.

"If you can do that, you can presumably condense matter. Consult your ballistics section; I think they'll agree that a shot whose inertia was so large compared to its size would permit tremendous accuracy over very long distances. My view is that it was designed to expand to its normal volume when it struck the outer wall of the pipe. Moreover, it was made of some volatile compound that dissipated in the escaping gas—perhaps a substance soluble in chlorine but not in ordinary air. This accounts for your detectives not finding it when they came on the scene.

"And another thing. This ties in with what I told you before—that the Starhomers are connected with the League. As far as we know, only on Starhome would anyone have the ability to make such bullets."

Klabund was looking almost happy now. "Mr Vincent, I'm eternally grateful to you. A special kind of gun sounds like something concrete to try and trace—much more solid than an influx of money or propaganda, which is what we're hunting for right now. I—I'm sorry I lost my temper with you."

"And I'm sorry to have pulled rank on you," I countered.

"Oh, I understand you're feeling the strain, same as I am. I don't imagine the attempt on your life helped any. By the way"—he glanced at something off-screen, and gave a wry smile—"we've got the man who supplied Castle with the parasite."

"That was fast work. Who was it?"

"One of the Fellows in the Cambridge Faculty of Medicine. Name of Aristide Scarlatti, an extra-terrestrial biochemist. As a matter of fact, when we picked him up he'd just initiated a new research project involving a friend of yours, who's with me now. Which of course is why I didn't want to be interrupted. Anovel!"

He swung the phone around, and there was the Regulan perched on a high broad stool, his back-bent legs hanging down the far side. He nodded a greeting to me, ripples running down his yellow mane.

"A pity about Scarlatti—he's a brilliant man. But dreadfully mixed up in his mind! He's pathologically convinced that my virtual immunity to anything which endangers a human life implies an insult to his own species. I'm surprised his psychosis hadn't been noticed before."

The phone swung back to show Klabund, very worried. "I'm afraid that's so. Scarlatti appeared to be doing his best to—uh—penetrate that immunity."

"You mean find a way of killing Anovel?" My head spun; this was the stuff of which we in the Bureau made our nightmares.

"Bluntly, yes. Luckily Anovel has been most under-standing about the whole nasty affair."

"Tell him that his—uh—employer on the zoo ship is going to find him a bad bargain," I said in a tone of forced lightness. "And ask if he'd care to come over to my apartment for the evening, if he's free."

Klabund relayed the message, turning the phone again.

"I'd be delighted," Anovel said. "May I have the address?"

I gave it, suggested he come at twenty hours, and rang off with my hands shaking. Immediately I called Tinescu, meaning to break the awful news.

But he'd already heard it.

"It's a disgraceful thing to have happened," he agreed. "But it was at least a Regulan who was concerned, not some more vulnerable creature."

"A pretty slim consolation!" I snapped. "What's a League sympathizer doing in alien biology, anyway? Try-ing to put his race-prejudice on a scientific footing?"

"Possibly." Tinescu gave a glance at the clock in his office, out of range of the camera. "Don't let it bother you, Roald. I've discussed it with Indowegiatuk, and the verdict is that now the harm's done we can only rely on Anovel's tolerance."

"He seemed amused, rather than annoyed," I conceded. "But it's hard to know what those beasts are thinking . . . Anyhow, I did the first thing that came into my head: invited him to my apartment for the evening."

"What's become of this woman who's been monopoliz-ing your evenings, then?" Tinescu grunted.

"Huh? Oh, Patricia!" I forced a laugh. "She's off to see her sister in Alaska."

"I thought there must be some special reason for your being on your own. Well, do your best with Anovel, but I don't expect much from your meeting."

"Nor do I." I frowned. "You know, Regulans worry me.

I get the impression that it's we who ought to be travelling in *their* zoo ships."

"Agreed! With their fantastic adaptability they seem tailor-made for interstellar colonization. Well, I must be off—dinner with the Minister again tonight." He sighed lugubriously, and cut the connection.

21

"TWENTY hours is rather a neutral time for an evening invitation," Anovel said deprecatingly. "An hour earlier, and one is certain that a meal is included in the invitation; an hour later, and one may assume the necessity of eating before one arrives. Lacking a truly exact knowledge of Earthly etiquette, and realizing that food suitable for my species may be difficult for you to obtain, I brought my own. I trust I don't offend the code of good manners."

"Not at all," I said. "Though getting Regulan food isn't any problem for me. I'd intended to call the Ark and have a meal sent over. That's one of the advantages of being in the Bureau."

"Not one which most people envy you?" Anovel suggested dryly, cocking his long head, and I had to chuckle.

I watched with interest as he set out his meal on my table: a number of sandwich-like objects made of a material resembling brown glass and textured like a cracknel biscuit, filled with a creamy substance as yellow as his mane; a globular fruit whose thick white skin was patched with black, which he broke tidily into quarters and dusted with sodium fluoride; and a dish containing a dark green liquid as sluggish as mercury.

"Tell me," I said, "is eating a social function among your people? I know it is among the Sags and the Ophiuchians."

"So far as I know, the sharing of food is characteristic of all advanced species. I remember talking to a member of one of your survey missions on my own world, who suggested it might be because food is such a valuable commodity in a primitive community. Once it's established that it is for sharing rather than hoarding, the first stage has been passed on the way to a developed society—in which co-operation is indispensable."

I nodded. "Sounds plausible. In our case, it would have been the hunter-family relationship which started the process; at Sigma Sagittarii, that between cultivating and breeding sexes."

"Presumably." Anovel trapped a thread of yellow as it oozed out of his first sandwich, with a curious sidewise movement of his lower lip. "I have occasionally speculated," he went on, "whether civilization could arise among a species whose nourishment is come by automatically—say, a race subsisting on solar energy and reactive gases. My impression is that it could not, any more than it has done among your plants—or if it did, it would be based on motives incomprehensible to us, and we wouldn't recognize it as civilization."

For a moment I was silent. I'd been inclined to regret my spur-of-the-moment invitation before Anovel arrived; then I began to enjoy myself when I discovered what pleasant company he was, and now we'd been chatting happily for an hour and a half. The mention of "incomprehensible motives", however, had cast me back to my original intention: to try and determine the alien's reaction to Scarlatti's horrifying behaviour. While I was still pondering he spoke again. He seemed to have no difficulty in talking with a full mouth.

"Of course, it might not have to be food which was the

essential symbol. It's a common denominator we take for granted, but you have had—so I'm told—societies on this planet which maintained a fairly high cultural level despite minimal co-operation between the members."

I thought back to my college sociology courses, and to the pioneering work of twentieth-century anthropologists. "Do you mean societies like the Dobu, where the members were insanely suspicious of one another's intentions?"

"Yes, I had that example in mind." He dipped his flexible lips into the green fluid and drank daintily. "Such attitudes are no longer socialized, of course—though I'm afraid they survive in individuals. One person this applies to is Aristide Scarlatti, whose acquaintance I made so briefly and was not unhappy to be deprived of."

"You—uh—you view him as atypical?" I ventured hopefully.

"If he weren't, you couldn't support this weight of technology, could you? I gather it's a truism in your psychology that maniacs do not combine; their communication is too meagre. In a sense Scarlatti is mad, wouldn't you agree? Racial loyalty is praiseworthy in itself, but when it's distorted into talk of divine right and intrinsic superiority it's—foolish!"

He sounded annoyed, yet at the same time clinically detached, like a doctor frustrated at the poor progress of a mental patient. And yet how could I know whether his tone and manner reflected his true feelings?

Not for the first time today I wondered why we weren't the ones to travel in Regulan zoo ships. Anovel's people appeared to have the mental attributes required for the invention of space travel: an interest in other planets and races, acute intelligence, excellent astronomy and astrophysics—not to mention their unique physical qualifications. In spite of which, they seemed content to take advantage of Earth's starflight monopoly and to permit us to maintain survey missions on their planet.

The official excuse for our mystification at this state of affairs was that we ought not to anthropomorphize. Regulan goals and ideals might differ fundamentally from ours; we might have assigned definitions to them which owing to loss in translation were badly inaccurate. We took it for granted that cultures of a certain type aimed ultimately at interstellar travel—our own, or the Tau Cetians'. Regulans had to be an exception, however well they fitted most of the prime assumptions. Certainly one couldn't say they hadn't got to the right stage yet—their culture had a *finished* quality, being tremendously stable and simple.

Maybe they didn't care one way or the other.

I finished my own main course and for dessert took a plum from the bowl in the centre of the table. Anovel had already eaten everything he'd brought, leaving neither crumbs nor dregs.

I was turning the egg-shaped yellow fruit round and round in my hand when Anovel pitched me headling into the situation I'd been postponing ever since he arrived.

"Forgive me for saying this, Roald, but we're a direct species. It's my impression that you are working up to something, and perhaps afraid of offending me if you broach the subject. I assure you any questions you care to ask will be treated quite impersonally."

I gave him a sour grin. "You have a damned good insight into our psychology, haven't you?" I said. "I wish I had some insight into yours. Frankly, I've been wondering how you feel about what Scarlatti did to you."

"Contemptuous," he answered. His soft mouth quirked into a smile, perched oddly at the bottom of his long blue nose. "That *is* offensive; unfortunately it's the truth. I don't, however, bear any resentment against your species for what happened—you're making a commendable effort to adjust to contact with other races, and an isolated incident is nothing to get annoyed about."

He leaned dangerously forward on his stool, making a

movement like a human stretching of cramped muscles. "When one is invulnerable, you know, one can afford to be detached about such things."

I suggested we leave the table—that stretching indicated he found the stool imperfectly comfortable—and went to the player to select a music-tape. Half-way through the task, I decided I was merely stalling, and if he was in a direct mood I should take advantage of it.

I left the player alone and dropped into a chair facing him; he'd sat down on the floor.

"This insight you have into the way our minds work . . . Is it because basically you think the same way as we do, or are you just magnificently good at empathizing with us?"

"Well, well! I've been in and out of your research labs for several months since I came to Earth; before that I was under study at a survey mission at home—and this is the first time anyone asked me that question straight out." Again the smile touched his mouth. "Maybe your species prefers to form its own opinions. But I'll give you mine for what it's worth, though when you eventually reach a view of your own it'll be more valid for your pattern of thinking.

"Do our minds work like yours? Yes and no. There's a difference, but it's not so much qualitative as quantitative. Let me see if I can illustrate what I mean from your own history . . ." He hesitated: the first time I'd known him to do so.

"I believe this is an apt parallel," he resumed. "What distinguishes yourself from a non-technical savage of ten thousand years ago? Mainly a change of viewpoint. When a genius arose in a primitive society, the order of his thinking produced the bow, the wheeled cart, the clay pot. Since then, though there's been no substantial physical evolution, the perspectives have altered radically. Your savage observed that the arrow flew further than the spear; conclusion, it's better for hunting. You, faced with the same situation, might think about kinetics, the lever, the conservation of energy—abstracting to extremely wide general principles. Yet you're both human beings, with the same mental endowment at birth. To use a metaphor, your mind has acquired a new dimension.

"Add one further dimension, and you get something new again."

"You Regulans have that—extra dimension?" I was on the edge of my chair with excitement; I was sure this was brand-new information, straightforward though it seemed.

Mane rippling, he shook his head. "I said the difference between our races was quantitative as yet. Only when we get to the next stage will we know what its nature is. We do, though, recognize that it exists."

Groping, I said, "Like getting at chemistry from alchemy? You've had hints that show there's an underlying general principle, but you haven't figured out how to organize your experiments and define it precisely?"

"Excellent! I wish I'd thought of that comparison myself. But before you ask me to explain what hints we've had, I'm afraid Anglic doesn't contain the referents to convey them."

I sat in silence for a long time. At last I said, "Why have you told me this, Anovel? I'm sure it's something our survey mission have never picked up, and they've been at Regulus since before I was born."

Anovel shrugged his massive main shoulders. "You avoid asking direct questions; you observe and interpret. This is because you are rightly afraid of knowledge you do not completely understand. But you carry that too far—you also refuse to accept directions as to how that knowledge may be safely dealt with. A precaution, over-extended, becomes a superstition—doesn't it?"

He rose in a single fluid motion and went to retrieve his platter and dish from the table. I jumped up in disappointment—I'd wanted to ask a thousand further questions, including the crucial one about why his species had no starships.

"Must you go?" I demanded.

"I've given you plenty of food for thought already," he said dryly. "But don't worry—I've enjoyed our time together and I hope very much that I may return the invitation."

"Yes, that would be wonderful," I agreed, mind racing.

"Then come and call on me at the Ark when you get the chance. I've promised Inspector Klabund to remain in this neighbourhood while he completes his inquiry into the rocket crash—very gladly, since it means I have more time to wander about and get to know the people of Earth at first hand. And the sponsors of my zoo ship are being paid handsomely for the loss of my time, so they have no complaints."

He put out his lower right hand, the delicate one, and I shook it warmly. For the first time I was conscious of an alien as a real person, and the feeling was strong enough to make me really like him. I wished everyone could get the chance of meeting Regulans privately—more privately even than by making them the centre of attention at a party. That ought to put an end to aberrations like the Stars Are For Man League!

Directly he'd gone, I crossed to the recorder and taped a summary of what he'd said. I planned to take that tape to the Bureau in the morning and send it without comment to Tinescu. I rather expected it would explode on his desk like a fire-cracker.

## 22

THE phone went. I reached for the switch and Tinescu's face appeared in the screen, wearing a grim expression. Maintaining a casual air, I said, "Morning, chief. You got the tape I sent up to you?"

"I just played it. Now we have another problem on our hands."

"Which is—?"

"Who the blazes is Anovel?"

I completely missed the point. Puzzled at how Tinescu could fail to recognize the name, I said, "Why, he's the Regulan who was involved in the rocket crash and—"

"Roald, for pity's sake! Do you take me for a moron?" He shoved back his lank hair with an impatient gesture. "What I mean is—what standing does he have? What authority?"

"I don't know that he has any at all," I said blankly.

"How I wish I'd done what I wanted to do, and given you the option of crossing to alien contact or getting to hell out of the Bureau . . . Roald, is it conceivable that you don't know what you've turned up?" And without giving me the chance to speak, he plunged on. "No, of course it's not—you must have realized, or you wouldn't have sounded so damned smug on that tape! Let's take it by slow degrees, and maybe you'll catch on."

He took a deep breath. "To begin with: what Anovel said sounded pretty simple, hm? So simple, it perhaps crossed your tiny little mind that the survey missions on Regulus Four ought to have worked it out long ago?"

"Well, yes, it did occur—"

"*But* you took it for granted they'd fallen down the way the survey missions fell down at Starhome when they missed the design break-through in building the *Algenib*. Roald, you can't equate the two. On the one hand you have a planet of inscrutable aliens, intellectually and physically our unquestionable superiors even if they haven't any starships of their own, who've never squawked at any proposition we put to them but have always kept us politely at a distance. On the other, you have a policy decision to conceal information on a specific subject. We can break down the Starhomers' secrecy bit by bit, but we've always accepted that the Regulans would let us know only what we could deduce from our own observations. And now suddenly, for the first time that I can discover, a Regulan lets his mane down and tells a human being—not even somebody in alien contact, but a casual acquaintance— their own view of their psychology, their racial goals, the *lot*. Now do you see what I mean when I ask: who the hell is Anovel?"

I did. I was furious with myself for not taking the point earlier. I said, "You think he may be more than just a tourist using zoo ship facilities to visit Earth?"

"More than just a tourist!" Tinescu went scarlet, and for a second he was speechless with the sheer pressure of words claiming utterance. "Roald, if you'd ever had anything to do with Regulans you'd know that those people do nothing without a reason. *Nothing*. I don't mean they're cold and emotionless; simply that they are the nearest thing to a totally rational being we've ever come across. I've sent your tape around to Indowegiatuk—don't blame me if she's in your hair shortly. I'd follow it up myself if Torres's programme wasn't claiming the whole of my time, because you may take it from me that if Anovel spoke to you so freely he wasn't just a private individual airing a private theory. Regulans don't operate like that!"

He glared at me accusingly. I said, "Well, I wasn't trying

to pump him, exactly. I'd decided, long before we got on to that subject, that he'd let me know what he thought fit and nothing more."

"Blazes, if that's what you can turn up without trying I don't know what you've been doing since you joined the Bureau!"

Hastily, I switched to another tack. "Ah—you said something about Micky's programme. How's it coming on?"

"If you hadn't been entertaining our blue friend, you'd have seen the first fruits of it last night. We put out a major documentary on the *Algenib*. I borrowed a team of top government semanticists to weight the commentary for us, and Port Director Rattray somehow conned one of the Starhomer engineer officers into appearing, though we couldn't make him talk very much. It was a howling success, by all accounts. Seems to have left the audience with a fine glow of vicarious pioneering spirit—sort of half wanting to go and congratulate the Starhomers on their magnificent achievements, half glad that they had to do the job and not us. If we can keep up the standard, we ought to soften our audience into accepting the pill underneath the sugar well within Torre's twelve-month limit."

He gave me a final scowl and cut the connection.

I sat pondering what he'd said for several minutes. What *did* he think Anovel was? The Regulan counterpart of a survey mission, perhaps? I was perfectly prepared to believe they could rely on a single individual to do work for which we needed a team of dozens of specialists. But at his age—one-sixth of Regulan life-expectancy—he couldn't be more than a student, surely!

On the other hand . . . how about our own prodigies? Micky Torres was little older than one-fifth of human life-expectancy, and he'd been one of our chief authorities on Starhomer social evolution since he graduated. He'd published *Stars Beckoned* at twenty-one; now he was *de facto* in charge of the biggest mass-education campaign we'd ever launched.

I decided that it would be illuminating to get Anovel and Micky together if the opportunity arose.

The phone went again, and it was Patricia. My heart gave a great leap of delight. She looked so delectable I wanted to climb down the phone and hug her. Then I noticed she was in outdoor kit and her expression was apologetic. My heart sank again.

"Roald, my sweet, I have bad news. I must cry off our date tonight."

"For goodness' sake, why? You were away yesterday, and—"

"Darling, I can't *help* it. I have to go out and shoot some trouble. The director at the spaceport—what's his name? Rattee?"

"Rattray."

"That's him. We were scheduling major precipitation for this area tonight at about twenty, and we have a beautiful fat airstream loading up with moisture over the Pacific algae grounds. *Now* he comes through and says we mustn't have rain over the port during the night—he has an ore-freighter limping in from the asteroids and they have to put it down as soon as possible because there's someone on board with a skull-fracture. So we've got to go and spill several million tons of water ahead of schedule. If you're going outdoors today I'd suggest you take a waterproof in case the clouds are still dripping when they get here."

"Won't you be back by this evening, then?"

"Absolutely no chance of my being home before the small hours."

"Couldn't you at least—?" I bit my lip, and had to laugh. "Now listen to me being jealous of *your* work! Let's make it tomorrow night for sure, hm?"

"It's a date. Same time? Wonderful!" She pursed her lips in a mock kiss and the screen went blank.

I'd barely had time to vent my annoyance in a few well-chosen words and dip into the conveyor box for one of the waiting items when there was yet another call.

This time—as Tinescu had warned me—it was Indowegiatuk. She was the oldest of the so-called "assistants" in the Bureau, but in her case the term was far more misleading than when it applied to Jacky or myself. In fact, she was a kind of deputy Chief of Bureau on the alien contact side. She was alleged to be over a hundred, but no one was certain; physically she could have been taken for seventy, and rumour said that all records of her birth-date had been systematically expunged so that she could evade the civil service regulations decreeing retirement age. Nobody wanted to lose her, and although she could have gone on to a post at a university rather than actually ceasing work for good, she preferred to stay with the Bureau.

"Roald, my son," she began, "I was with the first survey mission at Regulus before you were born. I did twenty-four tours there, the first two as a junior and the last three as comptroller. Would you mind telling me by what *right* Anovel breaks this bit of news to you and not to someone who can tell gold from brass?"

She was hurt. She did a good job of covering it up, but I couldn't mistake the bitterness in the words. I said, "I'm sorry, Indowegiatuk. It just came up in conversation."

"I see. And the purpose of having the conversation, I'm informed, was to find out whether Anovel was angry at what this copperbottomed maniac Scarlatti did to him. Is that right?"

"I'm afraid so," I admitted.

"In other words, you didn't feel that the people whose job is to handle visiting aliens were competent! You thought they might have overlooked something, hm? You didn't perhaps think we'd had an emergency discussion on the matter, run a score of hypotheses through our computers, and reached the decision that it was best left to cool down of itself?"

She didn't wait for an answer, but launched into an interesting survey of my immediate ancestry, and continued to Tinescu's, because he hadn't put his foot down and told me to mind my own business. I learned the technical names for several kinds of congenital mental deficiency and twenty synonyms for pigheaded obtuseness.

But at last she stopped, almost in the middle of a word, and fixed me with her deep-set eyes.

"That's what I think of you," she said, drawing a deep breath. "On the other hand, the staff analysts handling Regulan social assay data inform me that this leads to a rational solution for no less than twenty-three equations we'd previously tested and dismissed as mismatched to the observed facts. Did Anovel also tell you that he's a *kenekito-madual?*"

"A—what?"

"Blazes, why did he have to pick on *you?*" She sighed. "A *kenekito-madual*—the term doesn't translate—corresponds to what we'd call a 'government spokesman'. Such people are in possession of certain facts which they call *kenekito,* or 'crucial'. And they're relied on to reveal them when they see fit. This is the first time a *kenekito* has been divulged away from Regulus. And what I desperately want to know is why a *madual* has been sent here on an ordinary zoo ship instead of being attached to the staff of the permanent delegation! Roald, that beast has thrown more trouble at me than anyone in fifty years—I hope you're satisfied!"

She rang off with a gesture that seemed to consign me to the destructor.

It might have been a consolation to her to know that the very first item I picked out of the conveyor box after talking to her presented me with troubles of my own. A survey mission on Viridis reported that somehow two misfits had slipped through our supposedly foolproof testing for emigrants. A man and a woman who found even the undemanding pace of modern Earth too much for their lazy natures had jumped to the conclusion that—Viridis being pastoral and under-mechanised—they could emigrate to a life of self-indulgent ease.

It was an easy enough assumption to make in error; when I did my mandatory fieldwork I selected Viridis, and at the back of my mind I'd visualized an idyllic society akin to primitive Polynesian islands, where people could sleep in the sun all day and make love in the bushes all night. I realized my stupidity within an hour or two of landing, and had sense enough to keep my mouth shut about it. Viridis, after all, was not Earth, though astonishingly similar in a great many ways, so one had to worry about native weeds and inedible animals and irritating insectoids and bacteria which were adaptable to human tissues; on top of that, without machines everyone had to work far harder than on Earth merely to maintain a decent standard of living.

Two things had led up to this pint-sized crisis: first, these two hadn't had the sense to accept the facts, and were now going around complaining that they'd been deceived—and refusing to work like everyone else; second, someone had made a disastrous mistake in recruiting them.

So we'd have to bring them back. Free of charge. All human beings no matter which planet they were born on were entitled to the protection of Earth. That would make the Treasury annoyed. We'd have to re-examine our whole selection procedure. That would make everyone annoyed. If they'd lied to the personnel selectors, there might be a criminal charge to follow, so I'd have to contact the legal department; also I'd have to arrange for them to come off Viridis as soon as possible, which meant signalling the next ship to reserve them accommodation—come to think of it, the ship would likely be Martin van 't Hoff's the *Mizar* . . .

With half my mind I listed the steps to be taken. With the other half I considered several random associations. I found myself for a few seconds almost envying the Starhomers, who were so efficient compared to us; if they'd had to operate an emigration selection procedure, they'd never have cobbled it together from bits and pieces as we'd done, but planned it from scratch with elaborate precautions against failure. As they were planning a counterpart of BuCult now the necessity had been forced on them . . .

*Funny!* I shook my head. I could feel changes going on in myself. A week or more ago, I'd have taken placid, non-technological Viridis over driving, forceful Starhome any time I was asked to choose. Maybe it was talking to Micky that had shifted my perspectives.

How curious it would have been, I reflected idly, if the Starhomers hadn't contacted the Tau Cetians and we'd contrived to miss them ourselves. Suppose they'd developed starships of their own, and encountered men for the first time on Viridis—wouldn't it have been a shock when they moved on and found us elsewhere, too, living under totally different conditions?

Something followed from that, but I had no time to waste chasing it. I had work to do. Determinedly I wiped such speculations away and concentrated on the problem facing me.

## 23

A few minutes before noon I found out what had gone wrong—they'd revised the requirements for permission to emigrate to Viridis earlier in the year, and someone had assigned wrong values to half a dozen factors when programming the computers which processed the selection data. It was an honest error due to an ambiguity in the verbal definition the Viridians themselves had sent us.

So I buckled to and rewrote the offending section; then I had to revise every single reference to it in a fat volume of general instructions to emigrant personnel selectors, and by the time I'd done that the noon recess was over and I'd missed my usual lunchtime.

I yawned, sent the revised material for computer checking and printing, and set off for the canteen across the street. I didn't expect to find anyone I knew there—it was after fourteen by now—and by a wide margin the last person of all I imagined I'd run into was Micky, simultaneously spooning up soup and making notes on a document full of complex equations.

I said hullo, and he raised his pale face to me. Enormous dark rings had developed under his eyes.

"Micky, you look ghastly!" I exclaimed. "You can't have had any sleep since you got here!"

He stretched, pushed aside his papers and gestured for me to join him at the table. "I'm glad you turned up," he grunted. "Gives me an excuse to shelve that and it isn't urgent anyway. Just that this business expands into every spare moment like water filling a sunken ship . . . Go ahead, place your order."

I started; I hadn't heard the waiter roll up to my side.

"Tinescu tells me you've made a start already," I said as I chose my food.

"That thing we put out last night? Hell, it was a kite, nothing more. But it did go well. The port staff were most co-operative, especially Rattray and the supervisor who brought the *Algenib* down—Susumama. It wasn't the start of our programme, though Tinescu got so worked up about it he seemed to convince himself that it was. No, we've decided to build the first stage around the Tau Cetians to exploit their existing news value. I had a devil of a job getting bin Ishmael to make them available—he's still worried stiff that the League will have another go at them —but he finally agreed that we can have them. We shall play down the work of BuCult, I'm afraid, stressing the difficulties the Starhomers had in making contact—same general angle as last night's thing, presenting them as people doing the dirty work and doing it well. Then—oh, the ideas crop up every few seconds. Already we have more than the staff can handle. Tinescu wants to set up a special department—give it some neutral name so people won't deduce its purpose. Threatens to put me in charge."

"Who else? But will the Treasury allot the kind of budget a separate department needs?"

"Are you serious?" He drew back a little, staring at me. "Tinescu got us the first two billion yesterday. For an old man he has more drive and initiative than twenty ordinary people." A thought struck him, and he added in a puzzled tone, "How old is he, anyway?"

"I honestly don't know," I said. "He hasn't changed since I joined the Bureau—not so you'd notice."

"Was he already Chief of Bureau then?"

"Oh yes. He's held the post for about twenty-five years." I did some mental arithmetic. "I guess he's eighty-five or ninety."

"Was he very young when he was appointed, then? It

wouldn't surprise me—he must have been a brilliant man."

"He can't have been all that young. They tried having a very young Chief of Bureau the time before—somebody named Brown, who was only fifty-one. But the Bureau was going through a bad patch—the budget wouldn't support the work and the staff was going crazy with the strain. I believe Brown tried to kill himself. But it was before my time; you might ask Indowegiatuk for the details, perhaps."

Micky finished his soup and exchanged it for a salad the waiter brought him. "It's a curious fact, you know," he mused, "but we haven't even yet adjusted to our increased lifespan. I hear Indowegiatuk ought strictly to have retired years ago, because the limit was fixed when people only averaged ninety or ninety-five. We have this top-heavy load of people still active, still productive, whom we've shuffled off into cosy pigeonholes, and there they sit, chewing their nails and—*I* think—dying of boredom before they have to."

"True. One of these days we'll go beyond what we've managed so far. We won't be content with postponing the degenerative diseases we call 'old age', but we'll actually reverse the ageing process. And I daren't guess what this will do to the society of Earth."

"I've wondered about that myself." Micky folded leaves of salad around his fork. "When my father's mother died she was a hundred and twenty-four. She's a classic example—did everything twenty years later than people used to. Married at forty, children at about fifty, her first grandchild when she was well past eighty . . . Speaking of ages, you're young yourself for the post you hold."

"It's ageing me two days for most people's one," I said. "Yes, I guess I am on the young side. But the Bureau likes people whose ideas haven't petrified. Jacky's only—oh—four or five years my senior."

"Didn't it make for friction when you were jumped over older men's heads?"

"Frankly, yes. But Tinescu settled that in short order, and after the first six months I had no more problems. Why are you so interested?"

"I've been going into Bureau organization," Micky shrugged. "Seeing how to staff this new department Tinescu wants. I've never seen such a tangle of criss-crossing information paths—it's about time someone reformed it to an optimum pattern. You have to have fieldwork before you're promoted in the Bureau, isn't that right?"

"At least two years, and they like more than that. But people who do more than eight usually make a career with the survey missions."

"Damn. I have my eye on a new recruit, and in that case I can't put him where I'd like him—he hasn't been out in the field yet. Where did you do your fieldwork—Viridis?"

"Naturally."

"Minimum?"

"No, I stayed over for a second tour. As a matter of fact there was a girl I got involved with . . ." I hadn't thought of Vanella for at least five years. And once she meant more than my career to me. How people can change! I said, "Why are you so interested, anyway?"

"I just happened to notice you're the youngest appointee to such a high rank in the Bureau for more than a century. It might be illuminating if you looked up the name of the previous record-holder—bearing in mind that people live longer nowadays."

More than that I just could not get out of him. It bothered me all afternoon—Micky, like Anovel, wasn't in the habit of making such remarks without a purpose. But I couldn't persuade myself to send to registry for the personnel records; I might have to sort them for an hour before hitting on the man's name.

*Blast* Micky! I glanced at the clock; it showed fifteen hours thirty-one. I looked beyond it to the window, wondering how Patricia was getting on with shooting her trouble, and saw that clouds were building up in the west, wearing an ugly dark grey frown. It would take a long while to dry out that moist airstream. The rain would certainly drift this far inland.

*Patricia* ...

Oh, damn—here it was again. A little voice at the back of my head seeming to say, "I know something important and I don't realize it."

Normally I'd have shut it out. Yesterday, though, I hadn't done so, and the result had been spectacular: I'd been able to tell Klabund his own business, and they had found a hole in the airpipe from the Tau Cetians' quarters precisely where I'd predicted.

Being as vain as most people, I'd enjoyed that small triumph. It was too much to hope for a repetition; none the less, I shut my eyes and set off on the chain of associations which was now forming.

Where to start? Last Thursday night, apparently, at the Dembas' party, when she behaved so strangely. But I'd battered at my memory of those events many times before. Was there some other point of attack?

Something I'd said to Klabund ... about it being a Bureau habit to leave work at the office. In what connection was that? Oh, yes—he was trying to find out how the League could have known where in the Ark the Tau Cetians were living.

And suddenly I had it.

The knowledge brought me to my feet, almost crying out, a sickness in the pit of my stomach. No, it couldn't be! Patricia? She couldn't have lied to me; she couldn't have been angry with me for that horrible reason!

Yet it fitted. Name of disaster, it fitted far too well.

I sank back in my chair, staring without seeing at the window of the office. Cold ugly logic slotted fact after fact into place.

Patricia hadn't been annoyed at me for dashing off to help the Tau Cetians. She'd pulled away from me when I said I might consider making a tour in a zoo ship. She'd said something then which I'd forgotten: *let myself be poked and probed by all sorts of—*

And the phone had sounded and covered the word. But I could fill it in now.

*Monsters.*

It didn't matter that they were intelligent beings. Having blue skins and four arms was all that counted. *Monsters.* Why, hadn't she even said she was glad when Anovel left, though he'd been the friendliest and most fascinating person at the party?

Well, that was nearly unimportant. I'd stayed in human colonial work when I could have tackled the much tougher job of alien contact. Maybe I had some of the same instinctive resentment against aliens, myself. But just lately those who harboured such hate had turned from a negligible cult to a murderous menace. They'd joined the Stars Are For Man League.

And Klabund had wanted to know how they found out where the Tau Cetians were quartered.

*I'd* told them.

I remembered how I'd been sent to find bin Ishmael in G Block at the Ark. I remembered how—so casually!—Patricia had asked on the phone whether she could see where they were living from the roadway as she passed on her way to work. And I'd said in so many words that they were in G Block and she couldn't.

You couldn't see them from the road. But you could see them through the sights of a light rifled gun firing an improbably heavy projectile a fraction of an inch in diameter.

Was I certain the information had passed through Patricia to the League? No, I couldn't be absolutely sure. But I had told her where the Tau Cetians were, and she had been horrified when I suggested going to Regulus with a zoo ship—

Oh. Worse than that, even. Now it came sharp into my mental focus. I'd suggested taking her with me, and that had been the last straw. Then, she'd dropped the mask.

I put out my hand, surprised at how steady it was, and felt for the switch of the phone. Without turning towards the screen, I said, "Get me Inspector Klabund."

## 24

BY now the rain was only a few blocks away. I felt moisture on myself, and was bewildered for as long as it took me to realize that I was sweating with the tension.

Klabund's face went up on the phone. He nodded, and spoke surprising words.

"Good afternoon, Mr Vincent. I've been hoping to hear from you again."

"About what?" My voice was ragged.

"Say why you're calling, first." Klabund put on an expectant look.

I said, "Have you found out how the location of the Tau Cetians' quarters was passed to the League?"

"I don't know, Mr Vincent. Who did you tell?"

My misery must have been stamped all over my face, for he went on sympathetically, "I'd narrowed the possible routes to two. The more likely choice was via yourself; we found the lab technician who gave you directions when you arrived from the spaceport. That's why I said I was hoping you'd call—I always prefer people to tell me things of their own accord rather than under official interrogation."

I swallowed painfully. "I gave the information to a girl called Patricia Ryder. She works at Area Met. Right now she's off on a job, and she'll be away till late tonight. When you—when you do talk to her, I'd appreciate it if you could avoid telling her who put you on to her."

Not that it would make much difference. If by a million-to-one chance I had drawn the wrong conclusion, I couldn't see myself facing her again.

And if I was right . . .

Abruptly I hated Earth. I hated the beautiful soft delicious women of Earth; I hated its bountiful land and its rolling seas and its smug self-satisfaction. Most of all, I hated myself.

Klabund was saying something. I forced myself to pay attention.

"Mr Vincent, one of the oldest privileges of a policeman's job is to 'act on information received' without telling even the courts how he came by it." There was something akin to pity in his tone; I wondered if he already knew about my relationship with Patricia.

"And of course," he added, "you may be wrong."

With the breaking of the connection I felt as though I'd cut off part of myself.

How much had I really wanted to spend the rest of my life with Patricia, the person? How much had I merely reacted to the way she fed my vanity? I didn't know any longer. I'd never known. As though afraid of breaking a spell, I'd kept from questioning her on controversial matters—hell, the other night I'd realized I didn't even know the facts behind her orphanhood, which in this long-lived age was a surprising rarity.

All the comfortable roots I'd planted for myself were being torn up, one by one.

"Lord, but I've been a fool!" I said aloud, and thumped my fist on the edge of the desk till it ached from the blows.

I was so ashamed of myself I couldn't find words. What had I done to win Patricia for myself, against the kind of competition a man ought to defeat before marrying so beautiful a woman? The least that I could. It was the same way I'd tackled my career. Here I was, running a good department, a smooth, reliable cog in the Bureau, proud of having been appointed young to this rank . . . and what had I done in the past few years to prove I was worth it? As little as I could!

There must be something more to life than quiet efficiency, but when had I last faced a job that stretched me to my limits? I couldn't remember. I'd mastered this little corner of human affairs—our relations with placid, trouble-free Viridis—and month in, month out the work went through the department without snags or hitches. Until when? As Tinescu had said, until I began to rot?

But I was rotting already, if I could let Patricia make such a fool of me!

It was way ahead of quitting time. But the hell with it. I got up and went blindly out of the office, headed for home.


The worst shock came the following morning, though. Overnight I'd come to terms with my self-disgust. I hadn't figured out what I was going to do, but at least I was resolved to do something to get out of this rut. I was toying with the idea of going over to alien contact, even though it would mean down-rating, or perhaps quitting the Bureau for a sabbatical year and doing as I'd told Patricia I should: go to Regulus with a zoo ship. I was half afraid of doing the latter merely to spite her, so I was trying to evaluate my motives honestly when the phone sounded.

And there she was.

I'd assumed that Klabund would take her in for interrogation long before this morning—perhaps have men waiting to catch her when she returned from the field job, or when she got home. I couldn't prevent an expression of dismay from spreading over my face, and she leaned forward with a cry of concern.

"Roald, is something wrong? You look ill!"

I still felt like a traitor, even as my glib mind furnished excuses and half-truths.

"Yes, I haven't been feeling well this morning. Perhaps it's a hangover from nearly being killed. Ah . . . I may have to cancel our date tonight unless I get over it."

"Oh, poor darling!" And it sounded so genuine, no matter how intently I listened for the betraying ring of falsehood . . . "Look, why don't we make it at your place, then? I'll come over early and fix you dinner, how about that? And you can have an absolutely quiet rest . . . "

I didn't try to talk her out of the idea. What was the point? She wouldn't be there to fix dinner for me. She'd be in a police cell.

Yet I waited all the evening, hoping against hope that she would appear, flushed and indignant at the slur cast on her innocence, the recipient of an apology from Klabund for having to ask her all these questions. I did still want her. Or rather, I wanted for my own self-esteem to be able to believe I hadn't been so monstrously—and so easily— deceived.

When she hadn't turned up at twenty-one hours, I dialled for a bottle of brandy and drank steadily until I fell asleep in my chair.

Next morning, I felt terrible. But the central hurt had

receded to a dull black ache, and I was beyond further harm when Klabund called.

Mutely he held up to the camera of his phone a closely written document, and I read snatches of it, as much as I could stand. It said:

"Commitment order for sanity trial . . . Patricia Belafont Ryder . . . did knowingly and of malice conspire with . . . endangering the lives of certain intelligent beings commonly known as Tau Cetians . . . damage to public property . . . interference with the affairs of the Bureau of Cultural Relations . . . disaffection and subversion . . ."

The charges went on and on. I waved the damned thing away.

"I'm sorry I couldn't put you out of your suspense before this, Mr Vincent," Klabund said heavily. "But when we started on Miss Ryder, it was like turning a faucet. One thing followed another until . . . Well, it wasn't pretty. So perhaps you'd prefer me not to go into details."

"But—*why?*" I forced out. I meant: how could such foulness happen in such an adorable, beautiful head?

"Why should anyone join the League? She's been a member of it for years, incidentally. The psychologists are saying xenophobia, transferred megalomania, puerile trauma—but what it comes down to is that she hates the idea of aliens with the power of rational thought, and wants men to be masters of the galaxy. Did she ever talk about her family to you.?"

I shook my head. "She has a sister in Alaska—married, and I think with children. But she wouldn't talk about her parents' death, if that's what's involved."

"It is. Her father was with a survey mission at Sigma Sagittarii. He had an accident to his suit, and one of the local bacteria infected and killed him. Now her mother was herself a very unstable woman, I'm told; she was fixated on her husband, rather than having any honest affection for him. When she came home, she brought a Sagittarian pet with her—a gift from one of her husband's Sag friends, specially adapted to Earthly conditions.

"According to Miss Ryder, this animal was the centre of their home after that. The children were treated as secondary. The older sister was lucky; she escaped the worst effects of this, because she was adolescent—of an age to form friendships, and regard her mother as a person with failings, and so on. Young Patricia, though, was only five or six.

"I guess she too might have got over it. But by a cruel irony her mother was also killed. You remember the rocket crash the other day?"

"Of course."

"The last such was thirty years ago. And Mrs Ryder was on board."

Okay; there were reasons, there were excuses. In an age of early death, a child could understand it as a commonplace. Now, it must have seemed that unkind fate had singled out a helpless girl for unmerited punishment. No wonder she turned into a racialist. She must have dated the start of her suffering from her father's death, and associated it with the aliens who had attracted him to the planet where he died.

"Do you want me to go on?" Klabund asked.

"Yes—yes, I'd like to hear all of it."

"Very well. From the moment she joined the Stars Are For Man League, she agitated for deeds and not words. When the Starhomers opened negotiations with the League —she was at some of the very first discussions—and offered to help them with money and weapons, it was obvious that inside knowledge of the affairs of BuCult would make it infinitely easier to undermine public respect for your work by dirty propaganda as well as sabotage. You've already heard that because you'd stayed in human colonial work instead of going over to alien contact, which I gather is a more demanding job, the League assumed you were potentially sympathetic. She was assigned to seduce you and worm information from you."

I shut my eyes and squeezed the lid-muscles tight. I'd hoped random patterns might blot out Patricia's image in memory, but the effort failed.

"She was about ready to give up and report that you weren't after all material for recruitment, when the Tau Cetians arrived. I gather it was that evening she nearly gave herself away when you sparked off her revulsion by suggesting you both sign up with a zoo ship—is that right?"

"This is what made me suspect she was the one who passed what I told her to the League," I agreed miserably.

"Yes. But she was ordered to return to you, because this snippet of news saved the League from falling down on their first big assignment for the Starhomers. The rocket crash was apparently the League's own idea, but the attack on the Ark was—ah—'by request'. The plan was that the courier accompanying the Tau Cetians should report to the local chapter of the League, who'd already sent bin Ishmael a threatening message. You scotched that by having her sedated and put in hospital. They were all set to cancel the plan, or make a random attack instead, when Miss Ryder called in as a matter of routine with this datum you'd so casually let slip.

"Which of course saved the day for them, and made it essential that despite her reluctance she continue to associate with you."

I said bitterly, "Do you think I'm a fool?"

"For being deceived? No, Mr Vincent, I don't think you should be so harsh with yourself. She must be a consummate actress."

"But—" No, why the hell should I reveal it all to this near-stranger? Why should I admit that I thought nobody —no*body*—could pretend to such passion as she had shown me?

I'd been wrong. I'd been trapped by soft, trustful, stupid

Earth into a mistake of which I'd be ashamed for the rest of my life.

"You'll certainly be interested to know that we found the gun, by the way. And the supply of condensed-matter bullets."

What was that? Oh, Klabund was still speaking. I tried to seem interested.

"It was at the home of the head of the local chapter. And we found a supply of Starhome-made bombs, too, which our experts say might have been used to wreck the rocket which crashed. I don't quite know how to say this, Mr Vincent, but you've shown a degree of insight into this whole affair which is absolutely staggering. I suppose sooner or later we'd have turned all these facts up, but your brilliant deduction about the weapon used against the Tau Cetians . . ."

He went on, and went on, and went on. After a while I gave up trying to listen. It was only at the very end of his fulsome compliments that he said something which startled me back to alertness.

"As far as I can see, the only reason why Starhomers should be involved in this is that they're hoping to break off their dependence on Earth, and—"

"Inspector! Have you mentioned this idea to anyone?"

"Not yet." He blinked at me, puzzled. "But I must report it—to my mind, it's so important it ought to go straight to government level."

"Before you talk to anyone else about it, governmental or not, call my chief—call Tinescu. This is dynamite, Inspector, and I'm not exaggerating."

"I'll do as you say," he promised, and rang off.

## 25

So there it was. I looked at the heap of work waiting in the conveyor box, laid a small mental bet that there was nothing among it to lose me a single night's sleep, and won the bet.

I shoved the whole lot back, counted off three minutes to give Klabund time to finish talking to Tinescu, and went to the chief's office.

He seemed to have been waiting for me; at any rate, his desk was clear of work and he was leaning back in his chair, gazing at the door with pursed lips, when I entered. He indicated the guest-chair.

"I'm sorry," he said abruptly. "Klabund was just on the phone and told me what happened."

"I asked him to have a word with you," I said, forcing my voice to remain steady. "He's worked out why the Starhomers—"

"Blazes, that's not important. Klabund's an astute man, and something of the sort was inevitable. Torres wrote in a chain of side-factors to take care of it yesterday." Tinescu waved it away irritably. "No, what concerns me is the state to which one of my right-hand men is being reduced through his own silly fault. Roald, what possessed you to fall for the line this woman fed you?"

I said stonily, "Have you ever met her?"

"No, but—oh, forget it. What's done is done. I was going to tell you that in spite of everything I feel proud of you, and of my own judgement. It takes a high order of courage to sacrifice your personal feeling the way you've done, for the sake of an ideal."

"It wasn't for any such reason," I grunted. "It was half spite and half revenge."

"I don't think so. I think you discovered you couldn't stand a certain kind of person—a kind we as a race are very ashamed of, though the fault which made them as they are is by no means entirely theirs. I'm pleased. Which brings me to the point.

"You know, of course, that you're the youngest person to be appointed to your rank in over a century?"

"There was enough fuss about it when you promoted me," I muttered.

"Not enough, apparently, to get the implications through that armoured skull of yours. It may, however, have crossed your mind that I've held down this chair for almost a quarter-century, and sooner or later I'd ossify and move on?"

He was getting sarcastic; I recognized the danger sign and tried to make out what he was driving at.

"I don't intend to stretch the regulations as Indowegiatuk has done. She has unrivalled experience which would mean she was wasted in any but a Bureau post. I have no such excuse, and this business with the Tau Cetians has finally borne it in on me that I'm wearing out. So! This is no news, of course—I've known it must eventually happen. And I've taken certain steps.

"For example, you'll recall that before taking on your present position you were given certain aptitude tests. We already knew you possessed high intelligence, fast reactions, good emotional balance and first-rate administrative ability. What we were looking for was a rare and precious extra talent—the ability to draw correct conclusions from barely adequate data. Intuition, you might call it. Without a little of that gift, it would be hard to hold down any responsible post in modern government. Certainly it would be impossible to cope with the Bureau."

I suddenly recalled Micky saying that Tinescu had that

talent—he'd even described it by the same term, intuition.

"Well, over the past few days you've turned that talent on full, haven't you? Klabund can hardly stop talking about the way you figured out the method used to attack the Tau Cetians; bin Ishmael was delighted with what you did round at the Ark; Indowegiatuk is beside herself because you—"

*"Please,* chief," I said.

"Come to the point? I'm coming, all right. If you will kindly consent to get the hell out of your cosy office for the next two years and go see what's happening with the Regulans and the Sags and all the rest of them, I propose to nominate you as the next Chief of Bureau."

I didn't say anything. I couldn't.

"Well? What's got your tongue?" Bright sharp eyes transfixed me. "There's a precedent, you know. You won't be as young as my predecessor Brown. I know he broke under the strain—I saw him cave in, and it was pitiful! But he didn't have what you've got."

"But I haven't anything so special that—!"

"Oh, *shut up* and let me finish. You put on a front of thoroughness and taking pains. It's a front. It hides the fact that you're damnably lazy. I know as well as you that if you don't work till your guts burst you'll go the way Brown went. But I also know that right now, because of what's happened, you're feeling sufficiently annoyed with yourself to take me seriously. If I don't get at you before your shell seals over, I'll find you're too comfortable to make your own mind up. I won't fire you if you refuse the offer—you're worth something even operating at your usual half-pressure. But you'll spend the rest of your life in the Bureau wondering whether you could do better than whoever does take over my chair, and I'm glad I'll be safely dead before you start regretting the chance you missed, because by then you won't be fit company."

"Chief, I—"

"Get out, Roald. Take the rest of the day off and think about it. And you'd better come to the right conclusion!"

*Know thyself!* I didn't look up at the huge letters over the entrance to the Bureau, but I could feel them burning into my nape as I crossed the street, randomly wandering away into the city. I'd believed that I did. I'd thought of myself as a happy, well-adjusted person, doing a good job and doing it well, enjoying but not obsessed with the pleasures of life, having enough friends, enough girls . . .

Yet Tinescu was right. And he'd picked the only possible moment to tell me the truth: the time when I was so disgusted with my own gullibility that I'd found the resolve needed to alter the whole basis of my existence.

The *bastard*. But it was as well he'd seized the chance.

Take over the Bureau? Could I? Did I want to, even if I could?

Yes. Only in a negative sense, though. It wasn't so much that I had the ambition to hold the chief's post; more, it was that I no longer felt content to go on as I had done.

I'd been planning to marry, raise some children, stabilize my life for ever under a load of personal responsibility; the only other move I'd envisaged was one late in life, perhaps to a university where I'd lecture in Viridian sociology and leer at the fresh young female students from the window of rooms like Micky's at Cambridge. Or, conceivably, I might have gone for a while to some formal diplomatic post, been nursed through a tour by underlings and gone home with a glow of empty satisfaction.

Ach! Now these half-hearted ideas made me want to throw up!

I was furious with everyone: with Tinescu, for confronting me with a choice I didn't feel fit to make, I was so confused; with the League, for bringing back a kind of violence I'd hoped Earth was cleansed of for ever; with Patricia most of all.

I was dismayed to find I hated her so much I wanted to visualize her in the impersonal setting of a hospital ward, while the orthopsychists rebuilt her mind to a sane, safe, stable pattern.

I didn't any longer want safety and stability. It was time I made some mistakes, even if I had to pick up the pieces myself. It was time I did something to test myself, to find out what I could do if I was driven to the utmost.

Accept Tinescu's offer? That was demanding enough, surely—first, cramming myself with two years' worth of data on alien contact, knowing I'd have to be able to argue with specialists boasting fifty years' experience; then sorting out the friction which would develop among the staff, making them recognize that I was in charge; and, of course, working out Micky's marvellous programme over its long-term span . . .

*No.*

It wasn't right. It was a challenge, but not the challenge I wanted. I'd already thought of something better. I frowned for a long time. Going to Regulus with a zoo ship —was that it? No, what challenge in offering oneself as a passive object of scientific study?

Yet I did want to get off Earth. It seemed bland and sickly to me now; I'd thought of Patricia as embodying its delights, and—

*That's it.*

How in the galaxy I'd failed to realize this before, I was never able to explain. I'd dismissed it; refused to take it seriously; come near to forgetting it. And it was exactly the answer I was looking for.

I took from my pocket a little card bearing an address. I went straight to the address. When the door was opened to me I put my shoulders back, drew a deep breath, and said, "I've come to apply for the post of Chief of Bureau which you offered me."

## 26

KAY Lee Wong stared at me as though unable to believe her ears. She was wearing another of her mannish cape-and-breeches outfits, but dark green instead of red, and her face rose like a pale golden flower out of leaves.

At last she said, "But—but I thought you'd hate us so much you'd never . . . Oh, come in, come in! This is the most wonderful news!"

I had been going to ask what she meant, when the clock on the far wall of the room caught my eye. I said incredulously, "Is it after sixteen already?"

"Yes, I've only just got back from your Bureau. Sit down please! Roald, I can't tell you how glad I am that you're going to accept!"

I must have wandered, lost in thought, for hours on end. Well, it wasn't so surprising; I shrugged and went back to the question of a moment ago.

"Did you say you thought I'd hate you? You mean Star-home?"

"Well, after what we did to you . . ." She bit her lip. "I mean your girl friend Patricia. It was our doing, wasn't it?"

"It was much more my own," I said. And then, after a pause, "What were you doing at the Bureau?"

She seemed unable to meet my gaze. Eyes roving everywhere, she said, "I was talking to someone I think you know, a young man called Micky Torres. And because of what he's been saying I've realized—look, let me begin at the beginning.

"I'm not a courier who came here to escort the Tau Cetians. And the tour of recruiting stations I've been doing for the last week was a cover for my real job. I was sent here because it was decided that a half-pint girl was the last person you'd expect to be a spy or a saboteur."

I said slowly, "Not recruiting stations. Local chapters of the Stars Are For Man League."

"Right." There was bitterness in her voice. "You must understand, Roald, how much we resented being treated by Earth as a sort of planet-sized sociological experiment. At first that's all we were. But when we started to do things like visiting Tau Ceti, discovering the people there, and building starships of our own, superior to anything you have, we began to wonder how long this had to last.

"It's nothing new. Micky Torres has been explaining it to me. In the eighteenth century when this country—America, as it used to be—was a colony of Britain, it broke away from its old rulers and went on to become one of the greatest world powers in history. We saw the parallel, back home, and we thought this was the only way the process would work. We laid plans to force a break and make you acknowledge our independence. The League was only the —the *hors d'oeuvres*. You've no idea how much trouble and ingenuity was spent on fomenting crises here. We planned to give you so much to handle in your own back yard you'd *have* to cede us our independence.

"And what did it all go for? For nothing." She turned her big sad eyes on me last. "Because your friend Micky Torres has spent the whole day showing me the arrangements you've already made to give Starhome not just its freedom but its head, to do as it likes. Roald, I never imagined such generosity—and before we'd asked for it, too. I'm ashamed. That's the truth. I'm ashamed of the things I was going to do."

"How did they find out about you?" I said.

"I don't know. They just quietly shadowed me the whole time I was touring the League chapters, and then today a polite policeman came and said would I please come to the Bureau and—and that's all."

"It figures," I nodded. "Having a few people in positions of influence at Starhome, who know the full details in advance—that's a sensible precaution. *Kenekito-madual,* as it were."

"I'm sorry?"

"Never mind. A Regulan term I learnt recently. Seems to fit the situation very nicely." I leaned back in my chair. "I can very well see how you didn't anticipate this treatment, of course. Out at Starhome, your society is disciplined, tightly organized and aggressive. It had to be, to turn you from a struggling colony into a new world. But on Earth, you see, we didn't start with the basic idea of co-operation. We had to learn it, very painfully, and came near to wiping the whole race out before we absorbed the lesson.

"Perhaps there's a kind of evolution among planetary societies, too. Starhome, founded on the idea of achievement through co-operation, will take over where Earth leaves off after millennia of achievement through competition. And after all, the greatest single co-operative effort in our history has got to go into the next couple of generations."

Kay was staring out of the window over the city. She said, "I only hope my people will understand it was strength, not weakness, which brought you to this decision."

A memory came to mind. I said, "I was talking to Anovel the other night—the Regulan who was in the rocket which crashed. The League seems to have sabotaged it in order to kill him. Since then, another fanatic had tried to murder him under the guise of making some lab tests on him. But his reaction was this—he said approximately, 'When one is invulnerable, one can afford to be detached about such things.' In a sense, Earth is invulnerable here. We've made such a contribution to human history, nothing can take it away."

"I wonder how far we'll go," she murmured absently.

Yesterday, savages hunting through forests, hiding in caves. Today, intermediaries between races under half a dozen suns. Tomorrow—?

We sat for a long time in silence. Finally I got to my feet. "Well! How would you like to help me celebrate my new job?" I exclaimed.

"I'd like it fine." She gave a wry smile. "If you don't mind my celebrating the independence of Starhome while you're doing it."

And somehow it turned into a very long celebration indeed. I was still recovering from it on Monday morning when I walked into Tinescu's office. I was wearing a new outfit Kay had bought me—a cape and breeches in black with a narrow silver stripe, much more dashing than the kind of thing I usually chose—and I must have had an expression which signalled the change which had taken place in me.

Tinescu stared at me. He said, "Roald, I'll be forever damned. You've made your mind up about taking over my job."

"Yes." I dropped into the guest-chair. "I've decided I'd like to be a Chief of Bureau. So I'm turning down your offer."

I'd often wondered whether anything ever found Tinescu at a complete loss. This did. But it wasn't for long. His eyes grew round and his lips pursed in a silent whistle.

"Roald, you have more sense than I have. You're going to Starhome. Name of disaster, you're going to Starhome and I'm a thick-headed foggy-minded—!"

He lapsed into Rumanian. When he got his self-control back, he came around the desk, clapped me on the back, laughed, swore again and strode back to his own chair.

"How I came to overlook it I shall never know. What's

the point of putting the best available man into this Bureau when we've already agreed to hand over control to the Starhomers as fast as possible?" He laughed again until he had to wipe his watering eyes. I found myself hoping I'd acquire that facility to mock my own shortsightedness.

"What kicked you into it, anyway?" he demanded suddenly. "Going to marry the Starhomer girl on the rebound, hey?"

*Might be a good idea, at that* . . . But outwardly I matched his sarcastic tone. "Chief, you know as well as I do people don't marry on Starhome. They have cohabitation contracts.

"Mph. Excellent idea in theory—makes sure the children have a stable home. But always sounded cold and clinical to me. Well! How are we going to tackle this? Strictly, you won't be fit for the job till you've done this stint in alien contact I was going to insist on if you stayed here; however, the first job of the Starhome BuCult is confined to human relations—this programme of Micky's—so you can tackle the rest when the new bureau is being staffed up in a few years from now. Suppose we call on Charisse Wasawati, shall we? She can handle your job provided we haven't upset her too much by complaining that she failed to monitor her technical assay data from Starhome. Matter of fact, why shouldn't you just exchange jobs for the time being? No point in making a public announcement about a rival bureau till Micky's got his plans properly under way. Yes, we'll post you out as *pro-tem.* relief comptroller. I think. Have to take a few of the staff out there into our confidence, of course . . . "

He had it cut and dried within ten minutes, but I was still impatient. There was someone else I had to go and see, and ask some very very important questions of.

He was at home. Like Tinescu, I had the impression he was waiting for me. His room was in the staff quarters of the

Ark, for he needed no special provisions to make life tolerable. Over the annunciator his voice was soft and emotionless.

"Good morning, Roald. How nice of you to call. Come in."

I entered the room. Anovel was perched on a Regulan stool, his feet resting on the floor behind him, watching a TV screen on which a newscaster was just announcing the dissolution of the Stars Are For Man League for complicity in murder and attempted murder.

"May I finish watching the programme?" he murmured. "There is to be an interview with your Minister of Extra-Terrestrial Affairs."

"Please! I'd like to see it myself." I moved as quietly as I could to take one of the chairs he kept for human visitors.

Capra came on the screen within seconds. He didn't address himself to the interviewer, but turned to the camera and spoke directly to the mass audience.

"Yes, I'm very glad the League is to be banned. And I don't say that only because they've stooped to crimes I never thought we would see on Earth again. I'm glad for the sake of the other people—other *people,* regardless of their bodily form—who have so much to offer us in fields like psychology . . . and biology . . . and whom the League regarded as nothing more than animals. You may have seen their propaganda." He held up something I recognized: the cartoon I'd found in my conveyor box the morning the Tau Cetians arrived. "Robbing the store of human knowledge! Nonsense! I'm sure there are people listening to me who owe their lives to what the Sigma Sagittarians have taught us about genetics and the artificial manipulation of cells, and there may be some too who—"

Anovel's blue hand fell to the switch, and he uttered a sound like a sigh.

"Yes, Roald?" he said, swivelling around to face me.

"The other night," I began carefully, "you told me something about Regulans which—according to Indowegiatuk—wouldn't have said without a purpose. She concludes from this that you're no mere tourist travelling by zoo ship because that's the easiest way. She says you're a *kenekito-madual*."

"This is a self-defining truth," Anovel agreed.

"Everyone concerned with Regulan contact work is now beating his brains out trying to decide why you should have been sent here to divulge this particular *kenekito*. I think they're on the wrong track. It seems logical to me that there are two sides to your job. As well as divulging crucial facts, a *madual* must presumably also acquire them."

"Proceed. So far your logic is flawless." There was a ring of irony in the words. I took a deep breath, for here was where I really went off the deep end.

"After you left Jacky Demba's party, Helga Micallef called you 'a lovely piece of design'. More recently, my chief—Tinescu—commented that you were tailor-made for interstellar colonization because of your amazing adaptability. In fact, everyone up to and including Indowegiatuk thinks that it's you, rather than we, who should have invented starflight and why the hell didn't you? So far, the custom has been to dismiss the problem as anthropocentric, and attribute to you ideals which don't include that line of development.

"But then it occurred to me to wonder what would have happened if the Tau Cetians had built starships before we contacted them, and discovered men at Viridis without learning of the parent society on Earth."

Anovel listened, blue head on one side, like a statue.

I chose my final words with care. "There's only one explanation. You should have developed starflight. You *did* develop starflight. Therefore you're not a Regulan at all. You're a colonist."

The typical sad-looking smile quirked Anovel's lips. "Continue!" he invited.

"You want more? Very well. You *were* tailor-made for interstellar colonization. No single world could evolve such an adaptable species. You're an artifically created optimum life-form."

Anovel was still apparently waiting for more. I cast about in my mind, and suddenly I thought I had it. I said, "Have you decided it's time for us to know?"

"Not quite. Not *quite* yet. As you surmised, though, I am here to gather facts, and what I've learned suggests that the event will take place well within your lifetime. I've detected a subtle change in the content of your broadcasts lately, which indicates that you of Earth may be preparing to cede supremacy to Starhome. If you're capable of doing that without hysteria, you may well be capable of accepting the existence of a race which has had starflight for fifteen thousand years."

"That long?" I whispered. "Why—I'm amazed you can treat us the way you do!"

"Oh, we have great respect for you. We've come further than you have on our own, but you've reached your present level faster than we did. Together, we should make an impressive combination."

"Where did you come from originally?"

"A long time ago, we evolved around a star you can't see from Earth—it's buried in the Milky Way."

"How is it we've never met any of your ships? I don't mean in space—that's an astronomical coincidence. I mean visiting Regulus."

"Until the *madual* think it wise, no more of our ships are calling at Regulus. Not that this worries us—I told you that our concern is to add the next dimension to our intellect, as it were. Doing things, going places, belong to an earlier day. But of course other colonies have other goals

—perhaps as far from ours as the Starhomers' are from the Viridians'."

"How many of them?" I demanded.

"Many hundreds." But this didn't seem to interest Anovel much; he shifted on his stool and eyed me curiously.

"In a sense you're *madual* yourself, you know. At any rate you fit our concept more closely than any other of your species I've met. I think your *kenekito* concerns the matter I referred to just now—transfer of dominance to Starhome. Am I right?"

I hesitated. With a touch of pique, he added, "Roald, I *am* one who is trusted with such things!"

Granted. So I overcame my reluctance and told him the full story.

"I wish you all success," he said when I was done. "If it goes well, you should be ready to meet us in fifty years. My compliments!"

He rose and held out his hand; I did the same.

"But before you leave," he said, "there is one thing I have to do. I regret the necessity, but . . . There is a third side to the word of a *madual*. And that is the suppression of *kenekito* not yet ripe to be divulged."

Some force seemed to flow from the hand which touched mine, and instantly I forgot what I had learned.

# EPILOGUE

Roald Vincent, Director-in-chief of the Interstellar Cultural Exchange, chairman of the Multiracial Board, ex officio vice-chairman of the Starhome Planetary Council, Fellow of the Starhome Scientific Academy, corresponding member of the Academy of Earth, honorary patron of the Sociology Society, fourteen times an honorary doctor of various universities under three different suns, folded his new cohabitation contract and slipped it into his pocket along with the pictures of Kay, his two sons, and his granddaughter, He gave a sigh of contentment. It was a good idea to try separating for a while when the oldest boy got married, and he couldn't deny he'd enjoyed his little fling. He was pretty sure Kay had enjoyed hers, too; she was still amazingly attractive. The point was neither of them enjoyed it enough. So . . .

Fifty years since their first meeting! In the old days it would have been a lifetime. But here he was, still vigorous —as he had recently proved to his entire satisfaction— and looking forward to another thirty years of productive work.

He gazed out of his office window at the world which he had made his home. It wasn't Earth. But in some ways it was better than Earth, and he could take some of the credit for it becoming so.

His mind roamed. Some of the changes that had taken place were fantastic, considering it was only half a century. Who'd have expected Shvast, the little interpreter, to be elected first planetary president of Tau Ceti Four?

*A world government and a world language already—and probably, before he died, he'd see a starship built by Tau Cetians landing at the port here.*

*And Jacky Demba becoming Minister of Extra-Terrestrial Affairs, back Earthside! Attending Tinescu's funeral, laying the wreath of Starhome lilies which Roald had been able to send when the new Starhomer ships cut interstellar freight charges from prohibitive to merely exorbitant . . .*

*And Micky Torres, of course. When they'd finally revealed the secret masked by the innocuously-titled Department of Pan-human Relations, there had been that fantastic write-in campaign which almost made him President of Earth against his will. Ridiculous! President of Earth at forty? But he would have refused the job anyway; his eyes were set on something much more crucial, and here it was turning up at last. He'd been behind the scenes all the time when they set up the Multiracial Board, had masterminded its progress for more than a decade, and now was resigned to coming into the spotlight, for the other races would accept no one else as chairman when they turned it into the brand-new Council of Worlds.*

*Roald was glad that with the dissolution of the old Board he'd have one less job on his shoulders. He'd never had Micky's gift for cramming his time to the uttermost. His eyes lingered on a row of books in a place of honour under he window; three novels, three authoritative texts on social evolution, and a classic study of the forces responsible for war, all bearing the proud name of Miguel de Madrigal de la Altas Torres.*

*When the hell did Micky fit all of it in?*

*He was roused from his reverie by the phone. The face of one of his aides appeared on the screen, taut with excitement.*

*"What is it, Wegener?" he grunted.*

*"Sir, there's a general alert been signalled!"*

"What?" Roald sat bolt upright. "Why in the galaxy a general alert?"

"As far as I can learn, sir, it's due to an unidentified ship. The Alcor broached normal half an hour ago and a few minutes later beamed in a message about some strange ship heading into the system from the direction of Galactic Centre. There aren't supposed to be any of our ships in that area, certainly not under sublight drive. Director, it must be an alien ship!"

Roald sat rock-still. In a single instant his mind had been snapped back fifty years, and he remembered.

By what miraculous insight into human psychology Anovel had worked his trick, Roald dared not guess. But he bore no resentment; fifty years he had said, and fifty years were up, and here they were: those who had had starflight for fifteen millennia . . .

"Director!" Wegener was shouting from the phone. "Are you all right?"

"Hm? Oh, I'm sorry, Wegener, I was just thinking. The Alcor is Master van't Hoff's ship, isn't she? How odd that he should have been the one. Well, stranger things have happened, I guess. Do a couple of things for me, please: have this ridiculous general alert cancelled, and call the port and ask Director Rosenbaum to lay on a ship for me. I think I deserve to be on the reception committee after all this time."

He added the last sentence almost under his breath, but Wegener wouldn't have heard it anyway. He had turned away from the phone in response to another call, and now the mikes were picking up only confused fragments.

"No, that's absurd . . . can't be true . . . van't Hoff must have blown his generators . . . but Regulans? Are you sure they're Regulans?"

"Wegener!" Roald snapped.

"Sir, this is crazy!" Wegener cried, facing the phone

again. "The Alcor says the aliens are signalling in Anglic on our standard band, and—but it's impossible!"

"What?"

"For one thing," Wegener complained, "they're asking for you, and for another the Alcor says they look like Regulans. But Regulans don't have starships!"

"No, they're not Regulans," Roald said calmly. "Not exactly. But since they're asking to speak to me, it might be civil to try and rig a circuit for them."

Wegener rolled his eyes and made as though to clench his fists against his temples, but he was used to doing incomprehensible things for Roald, and since they usually turned out well in the long run he complied from habit.

Abruptly the connection was made, and there in the screen was a long blue head with a rippling yellow mane, so like Anovel's that the creature might have been his twin. Except that Anovel was at Regulus; no ships but human ships had called there in the century or so since the madual ruled that it was safest to keep back certain crucial facts.

Roald drew a deep breath. He had made several visits to Regulus and picked up a smattering of the subtle language. Using the most elaborate and formal inflections, he said, "We are honoured by the confidence of the kenekito-madual."

The creature in the screen looked him over at length. He answered finally in Anglic, deliberately slowing his words to a comprehensible speed—he was breathing fluorine, of course, and his subjective time-rate was far faster than the human in such an atmosphere.

"I am directed before communicating with your government to extend you an apology from a member of our species, namely Anovel. I am to tell you that he regrets exercising the madual constraint on your mind. He has watched you for fifty of your years, and has concluded that *the* kenekito *would have been guarded by your honour alone."*

He bent his long head in a slow, incredibly graceful bow. "Kenekito-madual *Roald Vincent*, we hope to welcome you at our ship. We await your arrival at your convenience."

# THE END

*Available now from Ballantine Books!*

## THE AUTHORIZED EDITION

**of the great masterpieces of fantasy by**

### J. R. R. Tolkien

### THE HOBBIT

### *and*

### *the complete trilogy*

# *"The Lord of the Rings"*

### Part I
#### THE FELLOWSHIP OF THE RING

### Part II
#### THE TWO TOWERS

### Part III
#### THE RETURN OF THE KING

**Note: This is the complete and authorized paperbound edition, published only by Ballantine Books.**

**To order by mail, send $1.00 for each book ($4.00 for the entire set) to Dept. CS, Ballantine Books, 101 Fifth Avenue, New York, New York 10003**